UNDER THE RUG

A novel by

TODD S. WONKKA

Published by Quill
An Inkshares Collection, Oakland, California
www.inkshares.com

Edited by Caroline Tolley
Cover design by Don Hou
Interior design by Kevin G. Summers

ISBN: 9781947848856
e-ISBN: 9781947848863
LCCN: 2018967133

First edition

Printed in the United States of America

PROLOGUE

I REMEMBER HOW much it hurt. But please understand that I'm not blaming anyone for the things that I've done. I never claimed to be a saint. I merely started out that way, sliding down the plasmic canal without sin, ready to believe in the world. Then, the lion came.

NATURAL PROGRESSION OF EVENTS

"WAKE UP, MOTHERFUCKER!"

Clive was kicking the back of my left shoulder, hardly the sensitive type. My response was minimal, merely a groan to indicate that I was alive. I was mostly naked, still wearing my socks and dead to the world, entangled with the bodies of two mutually disrobed women in their early twenties, both brunettes, both also wearing their socks. We lay sprawled and unfolded like skin-toned dirty laundry. Clive's kicking was just hard enough for me to confuse it for an enemy in my dreams, but not enough to pull me from my head trip and thrust me back into the arctic bough of the real world. He kicked again, a little harder this time, arousing the taste of metal on my tongue.

"Jake! Wake up!" he said in his signature thick and charred baritone.

Clive is my roommate and best friend—a most dependable cohort in the mastery of self-destruction. There is no gathering we can't pump full of mayhem, like a two-headed syringe of Deca-Durabolin thrust into the veins of the willing and the unwilling, a natural progression of events.

There's some recollection as to what transpired at the blast-off of the eventide, some scattered mental pictures in the middle, followed by an avalanche of void that fell in line with the sun's cascade—most likely some counterintuitive combination of beauty and calamity. But let me back up a bit.

7:01 PM – AUGUST 13

I HAD RETURNED home from tending bar at the Grand Lux Cafe at the Beverly Center. Clive and I were hired there together two years ago. He hadn't been to work in a while . . . taking sort of a leave of absence. I worked a rare day shift because my band was playing the Whisky at 11:00 PM. I rummaged through the cupboards for anything that resembled edible nourishment. Ramen, Oodles of Noodles, even crackers would have done. There was nothing but dust, a package of multicolored straws, two Sweet'N Lows, and a can of beef stew that was born there and would die there. My stomach was starting to turn on itself. I hadn't eaten much; a handful of french fries and a bite of an untouched club sandwich at work is all. It was left behind by some executive producer of shit films you wished you hadn't seen; he was on his cell phone the entire time, impatiently nodding and waving his finger at me—shitty tipper, too. Clive most likely went on a few auditions. He wanted to be an actor. Go figure. After that, he probably met with Bartolo, our drug dealer.

Bartolo is this sawed-off, stocky Mexican, drives a blacked-out Honda Accord. We call upon him often, usually more than once throughout the evening when we're carousing the degenerate cavities of Hollywood, beating the drum to a bloody pulp. He's always dependable and charitable with his portions. Clive makes the exchanges because Bartolo doesn't like me very much, thinks I might be a cop, so he keeps me at arm's length. I suppose I could be. He thinks Clive is nuts, which works in our favor.

Clive came home with the bounty shortly after I came home from the grind. I didn't hear the door open, still staring at the emptiness in the grubby cupboard.

"What up, boy?" he said.

"Hey," I said.

I looked at Clive. My hunger quickly started to fade at the thought of the zip and the drip.

"How's Bartolo? Still think I'm a cop?" I asked.

"Yut. Wants to wear your handcuffs. You want his number?"

I gave Clive the finger as he passed through the living room, tracking in the stale scent of a Camel Wides Light, the nagging hunger now completely bypassed by the anticipation of getting high as my stomach fell to my ass, indicating the impending shit I would have to take. I looked at Clive's left jacket pocket; he kept the narcotics there . . . his jacket, not my ass.

After a shit, shower, a few pages of Bukowski's *Ham on Rye*, and a change of clothes, we collided in the living room. Clive was sitting on the couch staring at the six snowy lines he'd cut up and laid out on our weathered tan wooden coffee table. We'd found it on Whitley one night, all alone on the sidewalk, four perfect legs. It looked clean enough, so we took it. Clive was using my Lux ID card to straighten out the curvy, powdered contour that lay surrounded by a disheveled mass of useless unread magazines.

Must have lost his ID card again.

I reached into my wallet for a dollar bill, a conduit to oblige the thirst of our adrenaline. A handle of Jim Beam lay on the kitchen's bar top, picked it up on my way home from the drudgery. I took a healthy pull, three gulps, all the size of a clementine, then picked up my guitar—a Martin acoustic/electric dreadnought cutaway, natural colored, solid Sitka spruce . . . a real beauty—to warm up for the show.

Things were moving fast, as usual. We'd rifled through an unhealthy portion of bourbon and bird-dogged it with a half gram. Just getting warmed up for the night's ensuing chaos, a bona fide Tuesday in the land of make-believe. Didn't matter that Clive overdosed six months ago.

"You're up, mate," I said.

I handed Clive the rolled-up bill. He blasted a fat line in one sharp snort, snapping his head back to feel the drip. I picked up the plastic bag.

"That's a big bagga cocaine." I looked at him and then back at the bag. "What the fuck? Bartolo give you extra blow to curb your appetite . . . so you don't try to eat him?"

Clive had put on a few pounds from when I first met him. Once in a while it required a dig.

"Fuck you, asshole. I ain't fat . . . I'm chubby."

He looked down like one looks at a puppy and lifted his bulbous overhang.

"Right," I said, my eyes the color of sarcasm. I reached for the tightly wrapped bill. "Let's have it."

I took a deep breath and dropped my face like timber falling toward the fluffy, ivory stripe.

"What time you setting up tonight?" asked Clive.

He got up and began to pace, grabbed the handle of Beam and pulled.

"We don't go on till eleven. Avi and the boys will get there early. They like checking out the opening bands anyway."

"They don't get pissed?"

"At what?"

"That you don't help."

"Nah. I told you, we had that out once. Never again. I market the band. I promote. They can set up for the shows."

"All right, princess."

"Fuck you, Dom DeLuise."

I'm the lead singer. I also do a majority of the grunt work. Flyers, e-mails, booking, haggling—you name it. In exchange, I told the guys that I didn't want to get there too early for shows, made up some bullshit about how I needed to properly prepare in order to perform. It was partially true. I do have my own system of preparation. But I never let them in on my methods of madness. None of those guys would understand. We're different that way.

Clive sat down, blasted another line.

"What's the plan?" he asked.

He was making more decisions six months ago.

"As soon as you drop five pounds, we can go to Reggie's up on four." Clive laughed. I got up, grabbed the Beam, took a pull. "You remember pissing in his roommate's bathroom sink? That annoying fat chick from Kansas . . . Debbie or something. Remember?"

"Yut."

"She was pissed. Fuck her, though. She was uppity, type you wanted to strangle. Actually had a dream that I did."

"Uhhh . . . okay. I don't think that's the *only* reason she was pissed off, psycho."

I took a pull of Beam, did another line. Clive grinned like the devil—but he always did—then did another line.

"Why else would she be so pis—"

"Wooooooo!" Clive interrupted.

I continued: "Maybe she was mad at Patrick. Poor bastard left in tears that night, busted out of her room crying like he dropped his lollipop. Or was that my dream? I can't remember. Are they fucking? I thought he was gay."

I'm not sure how Patrick Thornberg ended up in this unkind megalopolis. Perhaps it was because he'd washed downstream from Seattle, and the thought of actually seeing the sun—which he had only heard rumors about—was too comforting to pass up. We met him at the Grand Lux. He's not a good friend. We mostly have the tendency to feel sorry for him when we're not discounting him. He isn't any more lost than the rest of us. But there is something about Patrick that makes one feel like it will all end badly, sooner rather than later, a curious cat down to his last two lives, vulnerable in such a cruel, fenced-in, concrete meadow full of rabid, cat-hating dogs.

"Patty-Boy was as gay as the day is long. He got trained by Jose and Rob," said Clive.

"Jose and Rob from the Lux?"

"Yut."

"Yeah, those guys are wicked gay. What do you mean, *was*? Doesn't Patrick still work at the Lux? I haven't seen him in a whi—"

"Yeah, they're out and proud, all right, lip gloss and high heels, marching down Santa Monica during Gay Pride singing the 'Dong Song' with some guy's balls in one hand and a double-sided rainbow dildo in the other."

Clive flailed a reenactment. We laughed.

"Whatever blows your hair back." I accelerated up from the couch. "We should head up to Reggie's before we tackle the strip, yeah?"

"Yut."

Clive motioned for the bourbon.

"What time is it?" he asked.

I handed him the bottle. He lifted and pulled. I grabbed his other wrist.

"You cold?" I asked.

"I don't know. I can't feel anything."

I laughed, then checked the time on his three-inch-wide red leather band.

"It's 7:50. Let's go."

"One more line."

"Yeah, man."

We sat back down. I handed the rolled-up dollar bill to Clive and plucked another from my wallet, then poured two shots of Beam. We took the shots, then did the lines, responding to the flood of adrenaline by surging back up from the multi-stained brown sofa riddled with loose change, old credit cards, and sloppily forgotten pills. I grabbed the bourbon while Clive put the rest of the blow in the left inside pocket of his burgundy velvet jacket, a gift from me—I'd shanghaied the jacket from some Hollywood wrap party that I'd bartended a year ago. It was too big for me.

Off we went, out the door and to the right, blasted in the face with the unbecoming stench of mildew. The smell had been there for months from when Clive set off the fire alarm; he lit a towel on fire and held it up to a sprinkler head—somebody dared him to make it rain. We continued down the halls of intrigue we called home and turned left toward the elevator. Just as I was raising my right foot to press the up button, a sketchy young couple—guy and a girl—popped out of the elevator with their heads down, gnawing on their fingernails. They were both unwashed, blonde, and dressed in goth. Neither of them made eye contact as they scurried down the opposite hall like mice, characteristic etiquette for the seedy occupants in our domicile. We filed tensely into the polluted metal box, landing in the center, keeping our distance from the fusion of vile textures that garnished the walls. The smell alone indicated the possibility that you could catch some horrible flesh-eating disease from the boogers and grime that were smeared like a cake. We never leaned against the outer bank of the box, using a foot—or an elbow if we had on long sleeves—to push the buttons, still reluctantly.

"I did it last time," I said.

Clive sighed and leaned in with his right elbow, his hands quarantined in his pockets. He pressed the number four and the doors began to close. We looked at each other, our eyes admitting concern, and inhaled deep, holding on tightly to our breath. I thought of chocolate cupcakes when the doors closed.

CHOCOLATE CUPCAKES

I WAS BORN in Fitchburg, Massachusetts, a Victorian-style nineteenth-century industrial center that produced machines, tools, clothing, paper, firearms . . . gamblers, welfare recipients, drunks, thieves, and whores—a small city full of people with even smaller dreams, day by day inching itself closer to self-cannibalism.

When I was in first grade, I would walk to the house across the street from school after the final bell rang. I would wait there until my mother got out of work—Mom was an accountant. The tawdry pit stop was ratty on the outside, tan with dark-brown trim and an unkempt yard. The grass in the front had grown high enough to swallow the lonely rusted toys.

Inside the house were musty carpets and dark stains. The formerly white wallpaper had turned a smoky yellow and the air smelled of disease, puffing about like dust off an old couch. I tried not to breathe in too deeply until Mom arrived.

Who'd want to die in such a place?

The bathroom was the filthiest room in the henhouse. I only went in there one time, the first day. It smelled like death fell in a pile of death, and the tub was unclean. I'd hold my piss and shit until quitting time.

Why do I have to be here?

At any given time there would be three or four, sometimes five other kids not talking to one other, glued to the idiot box, watching daft cartoons. We sat on the living room floor, tried not to acquire any contagions from the piss-stained carpet, and gorged on juice boxes and chocolate cupcakes—the Hostess kind with the white swirl on top. I'd trace my finger along the spiraled white path, staring at those hardened sugar lines before devouring the delicious chocolate lump.

I never engaged with the others, only observed. My mother told me the lady watcher had kids of her own, two, I think. Her name was Elaine. She was lethargic, smelled like menthols and maple syrup. I tried to figure out which ones belonged to the tired woman. Maybe the one picking his nose and wiping it on his green corduroys or the girl with knots in her hair or the one who never ate his cupcakes, having overdosed on its invariable emergence. In the end, they all looked the same to me—grubby.

Elaine was scantily on hand. She was no bird dog—an overweight fortysomething with ratty clothes, usually a large blemished version of her Sunday's best. Her hair was light and stringy, down to her elbows, and unwashed, and her face was woven tightly together with deep lines and pockmarks. To be fair, she was never inhuman toward me or any of the other kids. She was mostly indifferent to our presence. Sad Elaine would walk heavy stepped from the kitchen to drop off the sugar water and candied treats, then off she went like a flight attendant on a long, turbulent voyage, disappearing into the melancholy kitchen. She'd plop back down at her weathered dining table, breathing heavily, exhausted by her arduous ten-foot beat. Then she'd light up another menthol and put on sad country music. She loved George Jones's "When The Grass Grows Over Me" and played it religiously. I wondered if there was a husband. It was hard to imagine her with one. If there was one, he was never around, and I could hardly picture him as a fit man. But who knows. Maybe he was tall, dark, and dapper and worked three jobs. Elaine could have been a former beauty queen for all I knew, now with less time on her hands to work out, less time to watch her diet. I don't think her life worked out the way she wanted.

I'm not going to let that happen to me.

She was doing what she had to do to make ends meet. It's what parents do. They make sacrifices.

Finally, Mom would show up and I would breathe a big fat sigh of relief. An influx of warmth would cover my body, blanketing the chill on my skin as she'd rush past Elaine with barely a glance, cradling the sum of me in her arms, the way only a mother can. I'd hold on tight, just long enough, without a word.

Please never make me come back here again, Mom.

Then we'd leave, I'd look up affectionately at my matron saint, and, like that, the last two hours of my life would come to naught as we walked to our pea-green station wagon, hand in hand.

"How was school today, sweetie?" she'd ask.

"It was good. How was your day?" I'd say.

"Oh, business as usual, you know."

"Munching numbers again?"

"You mean crunching numbers, hon?"

She'd smile. I'd laugh.

"Oh, yeah, right, crunching numbers."

We never stopped the routine. It was part of a ritual that neither of us was willing to let go. That feeling, when Mom would pick me up from Elaine's, was a feeling of rescue. Mom was never late. She was always there just in time, before anything bad could happen. That all changed when I met Kenny Harris.

WHEN THE LION CAME

MOM LOOKED BEAUTIFUL as usual, cloaked in simple grace, a red dress with patches of gold sequin—her favorite. It was a Friday night in the winter of '84. Mom was getting ready to go downtown, to dance and drink, a girls' night out with her old friend, Barbara Harris. Barbara came by with her son, Kenny . . . Kenny Harris, my ordained watcher for the evening, as my brother, Andrew, was sleeping at a friend's.

Mom was in her early thirties, her skin still soft and smooth. Barbara was the same age, but she looked more like an old mop who'd just been wrung out, spat from the womb of a rusted bucket. That never bothered my mother. She didn't judge. Barbara had a different upbringing than my mother's, her father a drunk, her mother sad from dusk till dawn; they moved frequently. She had Kenny when she was fourteen, banged some drunk at a bar one night, never saw the guy again.

Kenny was bigger than the average sixteen-year-old, six feet, stocky shoulders. His hair was on the longer side, greasy and unkempt. We exchanged quiet hellos, brief eye contact. I was a shy kid, at first timid around strangers. He was as well. Kenny wore a stained gray T-shirt with the head of a lion stenciled on the front in white. His light-blue jeans had holes in the knees, and his once all-white sneakers were as gray as a corpse.

Mom grabbed her coat and leaned in for a hug and kiss.

"Bye, sweetheart. Be good for Kenny. I'll see you when you wake up tomorrow. Love you."

"Okay, Mom, I love you, too. Have fun."

Kenny's mom leaned into his ear, said something quietly, as if it were the most important thing she'd ever said to him. He nodded in obedience. My mother was smiling as they left. Barbara was not.

"I'm gonna go watch TV," I said.

Kenny said nothing.

After a minute or so Kenny walked in. *The Dukes of Hazzard* was on. I kept my eyes glued to the TV as he sat down on the opposite end of the couch and took command of the remote. He flipped through the channels, stopped on some made-for-TV movie where pretty sorority girls were getting murdered in their pajamas. He took his shoes off, put his feet up, his dirty socks draped over the coffee table, wrinkling the white crocheted doily with every bodily adjustment. A few times he looked over, not really wanting me to notice. I pretended *not* to notice. What I wanted to do was go to my room, but I was afraid it would initiate a conversation.

"Where are you going? Can I come?" I imagined he would ask.

Kenny got up, went to the kitchen. I breathed easier. I could hear the sticky pop of the refrigerator opening, then closing, the unstable condiments on the door shelves rattling with each slam. He did this a few times. Every time, I'd hear the rupture of a tin can, a quick snap and a crack, crisp with the release of carbon. With every open can and slobbery gulp came a splatter on the blue tile. He'd return to the living room, fall to the couch, each time more aggressively than the last, each time smelling more like barley and hops. When the movie ended, he went to the fridge again. It opened, it closed. The top of a can was cracked but no splash, and this time he didn't come back. Some clock ticked by, thirty minutes or so. I went to the fridge, grabbed a Coke, sat back down, and melted into the cushions with one leg over the arm of our shaggy, old puke-green couch. I felt alone and free, like a solo vacation.

When I heard Kenny's voice, it startled me. It was loud but calm, coming from upstairs. My heart raced. The walls of my throat closed in, like a clogged toilet. I muted the TV, remained quiet.

"Jake! Come up here," he yelled.

I *thought* about ignoring him.

"What?" I yelled back.

"Come up here."

"For what?"

"Just come here for a minute. Come check this out."

He said it like we were old friends, and for a moment, I believed we were. I stood up from the couch, stared at the doorway. There were details in the framing that I'd never recognized before—dried paint runs everywhere.

He called again, more impatiently this time.

"*Jake!*"

I knocked over a chair on my way through the kitchen. Brandy, our adorable tricolored mutt—black, white, and brown—looked up from her food bowl.

"I'll be right back, girl," I said.

I passed through the kitchen and into the hallway leading toward the stairs. I was wearing warm socks. I slid my way down the hall on the hardwood floor out of joyful habit. I turned the corner and took the first step.

"*Jake!*"

"Coming," I said, quickly, nervously.

I didn't want to hear his *loud* voice again so I sped up and made the top of the stairs.

"I'm in here," he said.

It came from my brother's room, on my right, across from my mother's room.

"What's going on?" I asked, just before turning the corner.

Shock built to a crescendo and my eyes began to swell. My entire body shook. My knees buckled. I didn't know what to make of such a scene . . . obscene. I only knew that I was afraid. Kenny was stretched out across my brother's thin, torn blue carpet, wearing only his gray T-shirt, lying on his back with one arm behind his neck, awkwardly tilting his head up while his toes pointed up to the pale, cracked, water-stained ceiling. It wasn't that pretty at all. A shadeless lamp rested on the floor beside him—so bright. He stared at me with the ominous smile of a sinister clown who ate children, as I stood frozen in trepidation, unable to understand why Kenny had his dick in his hand. I turned to leave.

"*Stop!* Come here, Jake," he said, his tone low and shaky, disgusting with heavy breath.

I should have run, but I was too afraid. While Kenny was in the throes of an unnerving peace . . . and an unnerving pace, I, for the first time in my life, felt like I was going to die. Beads of sweat bubbled on my forehead and fell down along the sides of my face to my jawline, where they hung. Such heavy drops pulled me to my knees. It was only fitting that I began to pray. I prayed for chocolate cupcakes, the escape of them. I wanted to close my eyes and wake up at Elaine the sitter's musty old house from the first grade, tracing the coarse, candied line of white swirl with my finger, avoiding all that lived and breathed in front of me.

"Get up, Jake. Come here," he said. "I just want you to touch it."

I pressed my knees to my body, wrapped my arms around them, and sunk my chin to my chest. It took everything I had to push out a response, the words falling out of my mouth in a botched stutter . . . right into the meat grinder.

"I d-don't w-want to," I said.

I could no longer hold back the tears. The floodgates blew open. Snot bubbles spewed from my nostrils.

Please, God!

If I could channel my inner Bob Ross, I would stain the canvas with the portrait of a little boy caught at the mountain's edge by an angry lion not quite satisfied with his last meal. The boy senses his own death in both directions and can only wait for it. The lion stalks, the strain on his face ripping through the skin with each roar. The boy hopes for what any boy would hope for in such a situation, for his mommy to save him, or for the end to finally come, killing the fear once and for all—fear is the worst part of death. But the lion calculates, takes his time. He can't wait to eat, yet he does. He waits, because it excites him. The realization of imminent death builds up inside of the little boy with every intentionally slow step that the lion takes. The little boy knows what's about to happen, but it still hasn't, and he's left waiting, until the lion decides to tear him apart.

I felt Kenny move closer toward me.

"Look at me," he said.

"No!" I begged.

He put his dirty hand on top of my head, grabbed a palm full of hair; his grip was a vise. He slowly peeled my head up. I grabbed his wrist with both hands, let out a high-pitched screech, like a hyena caught in a bear trap.

"*Open your fucking mouth!*" he screamed.

I released his wrists and pissed my pants.

"Open your mouth, Jake!" He leaned in closer. "Or I'll fucking kill you!"

I felt ashamed. I didn't want him to say my name. He grabbed under my chin, squeezed my cheeks. My mouth popped open. I couldn't pull away. He put his face close to mine, stuck his tongue in my mouth. I gagged. Kenny stood up, angry, his hand still holding tightly to my hair, pulling me toward him. I closed my eyes, asked God to let me live, then pushed him as hard as I could. He fell back as a body shuffled behind me. There was a voice, a frightened voice.

"Oh my God!" said the voice.

Kenny shrunk. The look on his face changed from the lion scouting its prey to the embarrassed teenager who got caught masturbating by his parents.

Next time lock the door before you decide you want to forcibly mouth-fuck a young boy, asshole!

Paint that, Bob Ross.

Kenny backed into the corner near the head of my brother's bed, looking like a frightened child. He looked like me.

I turned around, caught only a glimpse of my mother's back as she ran.

Death punch!

I chased after my mother, wanted to calm her down, tell her everything was okay, tell her *I* was okay. She was sitting on the side of her bed, the phone in her hand and her head down. She sobbed through the sound of the dial tone, a thick, deep, chest-punishing cry. I said many things to her.

"Mom, it's okay. What's wrong? Are you mad? Nothing happened. It's okay, Mom. I'm okay."

She grabbed me, held me. It's all I wanted.

"I'm sorry, baby," she said, shaking. "I'm so, so sorry."

But it was too late. The ugliness of the night had sewn itself onto my skin, like a patch on a torn doll. All that love and loyalty that I'd felt in the past, that rendered me impenetrable, that guarded the gates of my soul for all of my life, it no longer seemed real. I remember how much it hurt, watching my mother turn and run. But I sympathized. She must have been scared. She didn't know of the fear that I felt. I wanted to be angry at her, but only because she wasn't there in the first place.

She would have pounced on him, right? She would have grabbed a baseball bat and cracked his skull. She would have grabbed a kitchen knife and severed him at the balls . . . right? Then you would have picked me up and held me right away, Mom. I know that you would have. You only ran because you didn't understand. It's okay, Mom.

Kenny took off when I went to my mother's room. I never saw him again. Mom called Barbara and told her what happened—what she knew of it anyway—and forbade Kenny from ever coming anywhere near me again. The two of them left town as fast as they could. I wondered who he'd babysit next.

The next day I woke up in my mother's bed, on the left. Mom was gone. The right side of the comforter was folded down to a ruffled triangle, leaving the trail of her exit. She must have left quietly, not yet ready to talk about it . . . Not that I wanted to. I imagine she stared at me while I slept, peering at my limp body, whispering—the guilt she must have felt.

"I'm sorry, sweetheart . . . Mommy's sorry. I love you so, so much . . . I'll never let anything like that happen to you again . . . I promise."

That's probably what she said.

The air conditioner was turned off, but the room was still cool. The scent of bacon, eggs, and toast got me out of bed. I opened the door, looked down at the floor in my brother's room, remembered Kenny trying to stick his tongue down my throat, then ran to my mother's bathroom and puked in the toilet. I cleaned up and went downstairs, hesitated halfway, afraid to face her. I was ashamed and wondered if she felt the same. Mom was hunched over with the phone to her ear and her back to me, sitting at the other end of the kitchen table. We never ate at that table. She whispered, maybe to my father or grandma, maybe to Barbara. I wondered if Mom would still be friends with her. A soft sadness in her tone offset the loud sizzle and pop from the cast-iron skillet. The sound of cooked bacon was loud and sharp, each crack high-pitched on the backdrop of an eerie silence that filled the gaps of each sentence. The elephant in the room was standing like a dunce in the pantry doorway, staring, waiting.

I better say something so he disappears.

"Smells good," I said.

Mom turned around.

"I've got to go. He's up," she said.

She hung up the phone, wiped her eyes, and walked over with a poorly built smile, looking past me at the stove. I was afraid of what she would say.

"Are you hungry, sweetheart?" she asked.

I felt both disappointment and relief.

My brother came home, seemed rather chummy, more so than normal. Usually it was a whack on the meaty part of my shoulder, or a charley horse.

Mom must have told him.

Andrew was a good brother to me, but not a day went by where I wasn't getting on his nerves in some way. But not today.

"Wanna watch TV?" he asked.

We watched Saturday-morning cartoons. The elephant was back, standing in the doorway, arms folded, a nosy look on his face.

"Seriously? You're just gonna keep ignoring me?" said the elephant.

"Talk to *her*," I said, pointing toward the kitchen.

Andrew couldn't hear us.

That evening my father came by to pick us up for dinner. He was a shadow of his typically energetic self. He hugged my mother longer than usual. They got along well considering his history of infidelity. Dad dropped to a knee in front of me, kissed my forehead, and wrapped me in the most incredible hug—I wish I could have enjoyed it. My father was affectionate toward my brother and me, but some embraces say hello, some say more. On our way out I turned back to say good-bye to my mother. She knelt down. The elephant stood behind her, shaking his head. He looked how I felt.

"Everything's gonna be okay, Jake," said Mom.

Is it?

She hugged me. I said nothing and we left.

Andrew moved past me and climbed into the back of Dad's orange convertible MG.

"You can take the front, Jakey," he said.

"Ummm . . . okay . . . thanks," I said.

We drove downtown to the River City Diner, one of those railcar-style, prefabricated ones. "The Gambler" played on Dad's radio—Dad loved Kenny Rogers. We parked right in front of the diner. A distorted reflection arrived at the same time, shone in the outer shell of stainless steel that formed the skin of the elongated canteen. The diner door jinglejangled, announcing our arrival, prompting the waitress at the service counter to wave.

"Anywhere you'd like," she said while brewing a pot of coffee. "Centerfold" by The J. Geils Band was playing from one of the mini jukeboxes that sat at every table. It smelled like french fries, coffee, and pie. There was a real sense that you were in the middle of nowhere in a small town just off the side of a dirt road. A family was eating dinner at the end of the car—a mother, father, two kids (one little boy and his older brother).

The mom and oldest son were quietly eating while the dad had one hand on the younger boy's back as he jumped up and down in the booth. At the counter was an older gentleman with a tan John Deere jacket, jeans, and tan work boots caked with mud on the bottom outer rims. His trucker cap rested on the countertop along with two singles and some change. A consistent steam rose thick from his cup as he hunched over to read the paper.

We chose a booth in the middle. Andrew sat next to me. Our waitress's name was Pam. Her hair was up. She smiled. We ordered cheeseburgers and fries and thanked her for the Coca-Colas she brought. In the booth behind my father, the elephant sat and stared at me with an impatient look, dribbling his fingers on the table . . . *flah-da-dum, flah-da-dum.*

"Not you, too," he said to my dad.

"Give him a minute," I said to the elephant.

Dad looked at my brother, then me.

"Jake, I wanted to ask you about what happened last night . . . with Kenny," he said.

My brother looked down at the table, picking at his thumbnail, frustrated. He had something to say, but didn't. One thing I knew for sure was that Andrew was my brother in the true sense of the word. He loved me, despite the fact that I was often a pain in his ass. He stood up for me. He chased off this kid once, Dennis Trench, a bully from the middle school. Dennis walked down to the elementary school almost every day with a couple of his friends after the final bell. He'd find me on the monkey bars or chatting with friends, start giving me shit, knock my books out of my hand, establishing his dominance for no apparent reason. I was too afraid to do anything about it at the time. When my brother got wind of my troubles (one of my friends must have told him), he decided to pay me a visit one day after school, showed up at two o'clock on the dot.

"Hey, Jake," he said.

Then Dennis arrived, and it was like I wasn't even there. My brother's eyes were ice blue. He had this terrible stare. Andrew was physically fit with a strong head, the kind someone would break their hand on. But he was smart, too. He could read people. As my brother approached, Dennis and his two understudies backed up. I was with two of my classmates who were also routinely picked on.

"What the fuck are you guys doing down here . . . at the elementary school?"

They fumbled over each other's stuttering returns.

"Just hangi—"

"Nothi—"

"My brother goes to scho—"

"Which one of you motherfuckers is Dennis?" Andrew demanded.

It wasn't but the opening bell and Dennis looked like he was going to cry.

"I-I'm Dennis," he said.

Andrew walked closer to him, his nose practically touching Dennis's, then pointed at me.

"If you ever fuck with my little brother again . . . if you ever set foot in this yard again . . . if I see you within fifty feet of either him or this place . . . I'll knock you into the middle of next week!"

That was the last day I found myself within a stone's throw of Dennis. Andrew was only thirteen when the lion came, but I know he would have never let Kenny hurt me had he been home that night. He'd have fought for me.

"Do you want to talk about it?" my dad asked.

"Not really," I said, looking down at the table.

The elephant had an interested look.

"Can you tell me what happened?" said Dad.

I squirmed, no eye contact. I looked outside, down at the table. I looked anywhere but my father's eyes.

"Nothing. It's fine."

"It must have been pretty scary."

"Yeah, I guess."

"Did he tou—"

I interrupted him, didn't want to hear the words come out of his mouth. I gave my dad some watered-down CliffsNotes, downplayed it, tried to close the conversation as fast as I could. It was too hard to talk about, how Kenny made me feel, to describe the fear that I felt. That was the last time anyone in my family asked me about the lion. They never pressed. Maybe it was my fault. I never gave them anything. I never told them that I thought Kenny was going to kill me that night. If he had just five more minutes alone with me, he'd have put his hands around my throat and squeezed, then raped my dead body. I never told them that I couldn't sleep the way I used to, that I was more afraid of the dark than I was before, for fear that I wouldn't see Kenny approaching. I used to feel safe. I used to feel that nothing, that nobody could ever hurt me, that my family could protect me from anything. I didn't feel any of those things anymore. As we left the diner, Dad put his hand on my shoulder.

"Everything's gonna be okay, Jakey boy," he said.

"Yeah . . . That's what Mom said."

Loneliness was what I felt, until I met Keo and Viet.

BEST FRIENDS

KEO WAS LAOTIAN. We were nine when we met, an awkward first meeting on the playground of our elementary school. He was picking a fight with my friend at the time, Matt. Over what, I can't remember. Our other friend, Nathan, wasn't doing anything to help the situation, so I stepped in. From the other side of the yard, I ran over. Matt was uncomfortable with the aggression of the situation, unable to protect himself. I, on the other hand, always wanted to be a hero. I admired the way a hero won in the movies, how they took control, how they held the power. But the reactions of a hero can be regrettable. There's the rub.

I stepped in between the two. Keo stopped. Out of fear that he would strike first, I raised my right hand and slapped him across the face, coloring his cheek rose-red. I was too afraid to punch him. That's a whole other level.

"That's enough," I said.

The assault stunned him, but he moved forward. I felt terrible inside the moment my hand struck his face, but I held that truth close to the chest as I was in the midst of battle, careful not to show any compassion, making sure I maintained the power. He said nothing, hands by his side, and kept coming, like a marathon runner dying out but determined to finish the race, fighting the urge to give up and cry. I pushed him backward with every step forward that he took, but he continued toward Matt. He looked right through me, a sad look, like a death. But I kept pushing, broke him down. After ten minutes, he stopped, looked at me. He was emotionally spent, finally realizing that the only person with more determination than him that day was me. Then he turned and walked away without a word. The next day I was ostracized by the very friends whom I had so honorably defended. Guess they thought I overdid it with loyalty . . . *Bastards.*

I thought about Keo all weekend, wondered where he lived, what his parents were like, if he had any siblings. The following Monday at school I saw him on the playground at recess, alone in the corner by the fence, sitting, drawing something in the dirt with a stick. *This kid probably hates my guts.*

I walked over, sat down across from him, grabbed a stick to create my own world in the dirt.

"Hey," he said without looking up.

"Hey," I said back.

The exchange was more substantial than it would appear, and for the entire recess, we worked together creating a city in the dirt. I can't explain how or why we became so connected after such an antagonistic first meeting, but an immediate friendship had commenced. Something about men and the heat of battle. When Keo introduced me to one of his older brothers, Viet, another immediate bond was created, and from that day forward we were inseparable. Keo also had two other brothers and three sisters, but they were all older except for one much younger sister. Viet was ten, two years older than Keo. My time with them was the most daring in my life to that point. They taught me how to roll in the cold, to live dangerously. They taught me how to make blow darts with a

sewing needle, some thread, and a straw. For what purpose, I
don't know, but we made them. They also taught me how to
sword fight. We would practice with bamboo for hours after
watching whatever martial arts movie we had chosen that day.
It was a wasted skill, however, as throughout all of my adven-
tures, I never came across an instance where I needed to wield
such a weapon . . . at least not as a child. Viet was the gutsier
of the two, more the leader type. Keo and I looked up to him,
but he never took advantage, never pushed us to do anything
we didn't want to. He didn't have to. He knew what we were
willing to do.

The brothers lived right down the hill from me, at the
bottom of Granite Street. It was the biggest, steepest hill in
town, great for sledding in the winter. In the summer I'd walk
down to the bottom of Granite first thing every morning, after
my Frosted Flakes. A long fence pole stood tall in Keo and
Viet's backyard, about fifteen feet high, went all the way up
to the bottom of Granite, just across the sidewalk. I would
climb through a railing and slide down the pole like a fire-
man into their backyard. The process of it encompassed our
relationship rather accurately. We broke some rules. We stole
apples from the neighbors' trees at night, rolled the paper boy
after his last delivery on collection day, things like that. We
were little assholes sometimes. One day Viet brought home
these little square white rocks. Ninja Rocks, he called them.
He said they could fracture glass, spider-webbing the entire
surface, creating almost no sound. You could then gently poke
through the web of glass and proceed to pillage whatever lay
on the other side of it. It turned out to be a valuable asset when
trying to break into someone's car to steal their stereo, or loose
change—my introduction into burglary. I enjoyed the high of
the fear in such things, and the necessity of having to be aware,
observant of the situation and its surroundings because we

didn't want to get caught. Valuable life skills learned through scenes of botched adolescence. I wasn't questioned much at home—standard stuff.

"How was your day, hon?" Mom asked.

"Fine," I said.

"What did you do?"

"Nothing much."

That was good enough for her. Mom worked hard. She was busy with a full-time job and keeping up the house. She didn't have time to see everything, and I was expert at hiding things, at lying, at making it appear that everything was fan-fuckin'-tastic. The way she saw it, if my chores were done and I was getting good grades, everything must have been fine. When I was home, I read books. She saw that as a good sign. I saw it as a way to escape the stench that the lion left behind.

Everything's gonna be okay, Mom.

Scraping against the nefarious sides of boyhood was exhilarating, for better or for worse. Those choices become much easier when you have sidekicks like Keo and Viet. None of us really knew what we were doing. We were simply bored, and our subconscious, our truth, took over.

We are who we are.

We were on a good run, undefeated in our battle against the world. Life was good. Until their father found a ten-gallon white paint bucket full of car stereos hidden on the back porch under some newspapers. I was constantly over there, so it wasn't the first time I had seen him get mad at them, never toward me, although I'm sure in his native language he'd made comments about my habitual presence. This time it was different.

Their father was as hardworking as anybody, blue-collar all the way. He clocked in at 4:00 AM sharp, six mornings a week, at the local paper-distributing company, assembly line manager, I believe. He was a quiet, stern man, but he was honorable. When my dad would drop me off at their house, Keo's dad would usually come out to say hello. They'd pass bits of small talk back and forth. The language barrier was a minor hindrance. My dad had more to say, but Mr. Raddavong was a very respectful man and thought it was his duty to come chat with the father of the young white boy who was constantly at his house, eating his food, watching his TV—essentially invading the space that he had paid for. Sometimes my dad would slip him some cash to cover my expenses. My dad was good like that, and Mr. Raddavong, though he never asked for it, was always appreciative.

After he found the car stereos, Mr. Raddavong stormed into the living room with the bucket in one hand and an Alpine car stereo in the other, his face the red of a raspberry wound. The three of us were all hunched in a lazy posture, watching a ninja movie. We sprang upright when he stormed in. I don't know what he said to them—he spoke in Laotian—but I knew by the looks on their faces, and his, that something bad was about to happen. The way they couldn't look at him made the room cold. They both stared obediently down at the floor, hanging their heads under what felt like an entire sky of disappointment. In their father's eyes, they'd done a great dishonor to the family name by stealing. Mr. Raddavong believed in working hard and taking care of his large family, period. He never looked in my direction, not once, while scolding them. He knew I was involved, but I was not his son.

Keo's mom, a soft-mannered, soothingly quiet, sweet woman, was always motherly toward me. She calmly but swiftly guided me from the living room to the boys' bedroom upstairs and motioned for me to wait. Two minutes later she brought me tea and biscuits. She turned the television on for me and left. I listened for a while, until the yelling stopped, then I waited a bit more. Finally, I couldn't take the quiet, the not knowing. I got up, shut the TV off. All sound seemed to evaporate from the Earth. I opened the bedroom door. A similar quiet.

Where is everybody?

"Keo . . . Viet . . . Hello?" I called out at a low, nervous level.

Nothing. I tiptoed downstairs, checked every room. Still nothing. As I was turning the corner in the hallway, past the wooden rack of house slippers that lay near the bottom of the stairs, I heard a dull, heavy sound.

Dthun, dthun.

It was directly above me. Up until that moment I had always felt safe in that house. I searched my mind for ways to be unafraid, tried to reason with myself.

They're probably stuck outside doing yard work or something.

Then, that sound again.

Dthun, dthun!

I flinched, but not enough to shake off my curiosity. I started up the stairs with chicken skin on the back of my neck and arms. I reached the top step.

Dthun, dthun!

It was coming from behind the closed door of Keo's parents' room. Their door was *never* closed. I looked behind me, downstairs. There was no one there. I walked slowly to the door, tilted my head to listen. I moved my ear closer to the door, almost touching it, hoping to hear something similar to the sound of crashing waves from a seashell.

Dthun, dthun!

I jumped back, my skin now detached from my bones. I looked behind me again. I couldn't take it. I reached for the handle, then remembered the story that Keo and Viet's older brother, Visack, had told us of the *Kasu*—a nocturnal female spirit of Southeast Asian folklore. He'd told a good story, had

us shaking in our boots. He told us how the *Kasu* would man-
ifest itself as a woman, with her internal organs hanging down
from the neck, trailing below the head, and that she preyed
upon thieves. I pulled my hand away from the door, thought I
heard something from downstairs. I listened again. Nothing. I
hated not having my back against a wall. I reached for the door
again.

I'll open it, pretend that I have to go home.

I announced my entrance and turned the handle. My words
had as much strength as Bambi's legs.

"Gotta go, guys . . ."

As I opened the door, I was hoping that the *Kasu* hadn't
torn out their organs as punishment for stealing the car stereos.
I'd be next. Anything else I figured I could handle. There was
only Keo and Viet. They were sweating and exhausted, both
bound to the bedpost with a never-ending lump of duct tape at
the foot of their parents' immaculately made bed—Keo on the
left, Viet on the right—both dressed down to their underwear
and their mouths gagged with red bandanas. Viet was trying to
adjust his position, attempting to lift the bed up enough so he
could get more comfortable. That must have been the sound
I was hearing. Both of their legs were also bound, straight-
ened out flat on the ground with duct tape across the knees,
ankles, and thighs. I thrust toward them to help but was just
as abruptly met with a strenuous grunt and shaking head from
both brothers. Keo wiggled his chin above the gag and spoke in
a voice backed by little breath.

"Don't, Jake," he said.

I was stunned. I knew their dad was a bit of a hard-liner,
but this . . .

"What do you mean, don't?" I asked. "I'm not gonna just
leave you guys like this. What the hell is this anyway?"

Viet managed to also pull his chin up above the gag.

"Jake, just go back into the room."

"And do what? This is bullshit. You guys need to let me help you," I said.

"No, Jake! You need to leave us alone."

"Just go to the room, Jake," said Keo. "We'll be done in a couple hours."

"In a couple hours? Seriously?" I said.

I couldn't understand. Punishments in my house were like vanilla ice cream compared to this. I would have been sent to my room, lost TV time, grounded maybe, but never tied up to the bedpost like I'd just been kidnapped and held for ransom.

"Here. Help us with the gags," said Keo. "Put them back over our mouths."

"What the fuck?" I said.

"Jake, please."

I dropped to the floor next to them, frustrated. I wanted to respect their wishes, but it was hard to walk away from what I was seeing. I put the gags over their mouths, got up, and walked out of the room.

I haven't seen or spoken to those guys in years. After I'd moved away it was hard to stay connected. It's a shame, so easy for people to lose touch with one another when you put even just two hours of distance between them. I hope they know that, on that day, all I wanted to do was be loyal to them.

7:55 PM – AUGUST 13

WE BURST OUT of the elevator faster than Clive could piss someone off. When we made the scene at Reggie's place, barging in without the courtesy of a knock, it was already abundant with the cast of the sundown's birth. "Welcome to the Jungle" filtered through the speakers, and the lights were reduced to a consolatory velvet tone. It smelled like vanilla candles, fresh weed, and the opulence of the fairer sex. Our arrival was met with inquiring faces. Some nodded, some stared, some looked plain scared, every one of them hiding something.

It was a typical Hollywood party—a melting pot of sweet, innocent, romantic stargazers with a dream and the most self-involved species of devil-trained citizens spawned from the depths of our beloved Earth. Hollywood is but a delusory terrain, 50 percent hunter and 50 percent prey, all gluttonous in their own way, that false glaze like curtains over their eyes, mainly concerned with whom they are going to probe in order to ride the fast track to fame or shame no matter what laws of decency said behavior will mar. After living in such an affected city for a while, it was easy to differentiate between the two pleasure-seekers. I'm not so sure Clive and I are any different. We have motives. But I like to think we go with a certain panache.

As we scanned the room, I recognized a girl from work, Niki Fine. We'd worked the same shift earlier in the day. She's a ginger, basic beautiful with a sway in her advance that exhibits her fondness of sex. She was cached on the balcony, straight across on the other side of the apartment. Niki and I hooked up a few months ago, made the two-backed beast in the warm effervescence of a Jacuzzi overlooking our pretentious city from the backyard of some record label executive's mansion.

"You gonna go say hi?" asked Clive.

"Yeah, I'll come find you," I said.

Clive started to say something but my mind drifted off to the night I had sex with Niki, and the encompassing harmony of Reggie's soiree began to fade . . .

Someone at the record label party was giving out ecstasy like it was candy; it was in a trick-or-treat bag along with condoms, a pocket pussy, cheap sunglasses, and a Matchbox car. Mine was a black Pontiac Firebird Trans Am, *Smokey and the Bandit* style. Clive's was a hearse . . . and Hollywood parties are fucking weird. We popped the ecstasy, kept the condoms and cars—and the pocket pussies—and trashed the rest.

The extravagant affair was kind to us—free booze, a wide array of drugs, freshly baked chocolate chip cookies, and plenty of drunk women to go along with the champagne and chandeliers. Twenty minutes in and my face was dripping. I sweat like a fat guy. I wiped across my forehead, snapping a splash onto the snow-white tile floors. Clive disappeared. He was probably off talking Shakespeare with a semicircle of partygoers. He knew how to command a room, sometimes aggressively, other times poetically.

I went outside to breathe the air and lay eyes on the sky. That only increased my high. I ambled into Niki's territory, caught her in an abandoned promenade. She was out-of-her-mind sensual in her lyrical movements, detached from all concern. She took hold of me without missing a step in her hustle, grabbing my hand as she spun away and out toward the city, then back into my arms, her lips pressing to mine. It was the perfect amount of wet. We danced slowly for a while, never prying our lips apart. Kissing a beautiful woman is something special. While you're on ecstasy, it's otherworldly.

We made our way to the hot tub. It was unoccupied. We took off our clothes while Warrant's "Cherry Pie" played to what seemed like the entire city. I got in first, then held her hand as she stepped through the steam and into the hot, bubbling water. We kissed some more. I was still sweating, but it didn't matter; we were both sweating. She backed me up, sat me down, grabbed my cock, and put it in . . . slowly. We couldn't help but be watched, laid bare underneath the stars, but we felt alone.

My flight to orgasm turned out to be one of those long, overseas aeronautics. The threat of not climaxing only relented when the ecstasy began to fade. It was worth the wait. The orgasm was mind-blowing, explosive. The force of its combustion felt as if it would blow the tip of my member clean off, leaving the apex blackened and frayed.

Before that night, Niki and I hadn't spoken much—a few flirtatious encounters, but mostly glances. She hadn't been at the Lux for that long, but noticing her was especially easy; she was beautiful without trying. Since the hot tub, we hadn't communicated regularly, although our relevance did shuffle a tad, merely a subtle rotation. It was more saccharine with her at the restaurant now, a few small, quiet moments. We shared something worthy of hanging on to, and it was somehow that much more momentous *not* to canvas our lustful encounter.

"Jake. Hey. Earth to Jake . . . Wake up, crazy!" said Clive.

"Yeah, yeah, I heard you," I said.

I snapped out of my hot-tub time machine, back to the present, back to Reggie's.

"I said try not to defile her on the balcony, you fucking pervert."

"I won't, asshole. There's no hot tub, and your mom's not here to blow me while Mary Magdalene puts a fist in her kitty."

Clive laughed while beating it to the kitchen. He grabbed two beers from the fridge, not at all concerned with who they belonged to. He came back, handed me a beer.

"Seriously, we only have a couple hours, so try not to have a go at her. You'll never make your show on time," said Clive.

I sped past his quip, kept my foot on the gas.

"How is your mother doing these days, anyway? Coming out for a visit soon? I love when she stays with us. Do you think it's weird that she sleeps in my room?"

"Fuck yourself."

"That doesn't come till morning . . . Don't you have someone to go recite Shakespeare to?"

Clive was notorious for waxing Shakespeare poetic when he was inebriated. It was a unique version of the mostly incoherent speed-reading of Hamlet, including aggressive arm waves, a crouching tiger, hidden dragon position, and the distinct mischievous grin of the Cheshire cat. Clive laughed, then vanished, left his beer on the counter. I could only assume he was escaping to one of the bedrooms—someone else's drugs were calling. Niki noticed me and nodded. I nodded back and made my way toward her. She was alone, listening to conversation. Her eyes shadowed me every step of the way, except once when she looked down at her feet.

"You waiting for someone?" I asked.

"Hey, Jake. How are you?"

She had an easy smile. I lifted the bottle of Beam in one hand and the beer in the other.

"Livin' the dream."

I went in for the hug. She gave back nicely, held on tight for longer than I expected. A throbbing desire to taste her pink, naked lips arose like high tide on fast-forward. Our profiles brushed, creating a stubbled, creamy white spread with light-brown cinnamon freckles.

Niki Fine was considerably fundamental—cutoff jean shorts,a tight white tank top and black high-top Chucks, loosely tied, and her blush tresses pulled back to a basic tight ponytail. To avoid making a scene and bending her over the railing, I opened with small talk—work stuff.

"How'd you do today?" I asked.

"Not great, made like eighty," she said.

"That's not bad . . . Short shift, right?"

"Yeah, I was first cut."

"Cool." I smiled bashfully, looked down at the ground. "You coming to my show tonight?"

"I can't tonight. I'm meeting Promise at the Rainbow Room. It's her birthday."

"Aw, no worries. Next time." It was quiet for a moment, then I continued. "You know Reggie?"

"No, I came with Janine. She knows him."

"Where is she?"

"Smoking weed in Reggie's room, I think."

"None for you?"

"Maybe later. I don't like smoking around a lot of people."

"Me neither."

I leaned against the railing next to her.

"You get Promise anything for her birthday?"

"Oh . . . no, not really."

She was embarrassed. I swooped in.

"Well, you can't go there empty-handed."

I reached into my left inside jacket pocket. Her eyes grew as I pulled out a pre-rolled joint the size of my thumb.

"Here, give her this," I said.

"Oh my God, it's huge."

"Thanks."

"Smart-ass."

"Just tell her not to smoke it all at once. It's potent."

"I'll tell her. Thank you." She ran the length of the joint underneath her nose. "Smells so good. I may have to enjoy it with her."

"I've got more."

"Yeah?"

"What time's the party over?"

She smiled, then blushed.

"I can probably get out of there by one."

I smiled. It was hard to resist asking her back to my apartment right then and there, but Clive was right; I'd never make my show on time. So, I acquiesced, conceding to the consolation in knowing that, by 2:00 AM, she'd be in my bed.

"Call me when you're done then," I said.

"I will."

"I'm gonna go find Cl—"

Some guy wearing a top hat and a purple bow tie interrupted by spilling his Sea Breeze at our feet. I grabbed Niki's waist and lower back, pulled her toward me and over to the other side of the balcony to avoid the mist of fruity Russian shrapnel. She smelled like jasmine. Top Hat apologized. I waved him off, then turned to Niki; we shared a smile at the expense of the drunken faux pas. It was nice being that close to her, and the jasmine was still there, so I kissed her. It was soft, and it was slow, and it said something.

"Call me later. Tell Promise I said happy birthday," I said.

"Okay," she said.

I was thinking that I better leave now before the moment was ruined by an awkward silence or her noticing my hard-on or some douchebag stumbling into the conversation with a haphazard Hollywood story about how he "got the part." Besides, I wanted to blast another line.

Somewhere deep within the viscera of my narcotic history, cocaine remodeled my identity, presenting itself to be the bright anthem of my towering nights and the lofty repercussion of my stunted, darker days—the purest Peruvian form of good versus evil, God versus the devil, or the devil versus God, depending on how you looked at it. When I was high, I was the truth awake in a pasture sardined with lies. I typically supplemented the flowery nose coat with liquid courage—bourbon. Together, they would form the pasty, yellowy-white shit show that was my life. In those few hours, when I was brain fast and word savvy, I would become either the trusted leader attempting to drag down whatever pack would follow me into some menacing crevasse or a disastrous wide-eyed bull in a shop full of fine china, emotionally and physically demolishing everything in my path, leaving a wake of relationships to mend. Eventually, dangerously, I'd fooled myself into thinking that I'd harnessed control over which path I could take, further exacerbating my desire to hitch a ride on the bleached bolt. I experimented with everything I could get my hands on: weed, painkillers, mushrooms, acid. But nothing ever romanced me the way cocaine did. Charlie Snowflake—that fine white lady. From the moment I bent down to inhale the pale, glittering invincibility through a dirty one-dollar bill, so began a great allegiance, and we danced to the ardor of bad decisions for a better part of my life. I wouldn't say that I was addicted to cocaine, I just loved the smell of it.

I went to Reggie's room first. Through the fog, I saw thin eyes and bad posture, about five people, but no Clive. My intrusion went unnoticed. I found it hard to believe that he would be in Debbie's room. Then again, Clive does have a way of getting back into the good graces of those he's offended—he's had lots of practice. I weaved through a dozen people as I passed through the living room crowded with plastic conversations—sugarcoated bullshit so grossly decadent I wanted to puke. I opened the door to Debbie's room, no Clive.

There were four people in the room, two guys, one black, one white, and two girls, one blonde, one Asian. They sat around a teak, oval, multicolored coffee table topped with a thick pane of glass. Creedence Clearwater Revival's "Bad Moon Rising" was playing at a conversational level. An unmade trundle off to the right, made up of two mattresses, one sheet, and a blanket far too small for the bed itself, more or less adorned the remainder of the room. On the thick pane of glass lay a bevy of party scraps and drug paraphernalia: weed, rolling papers, an opened pack of Marlboro Reds, a rolled-up dollar bill . . . some other shit. They looked up as I walked in. Both girls and the black guy nodded in acknowledgment. I recognized them. I wasn't formally acquainted, but I knew Clive and I had shared an elevator or two with them in the past. The white guy remained quiet, looked up, no nod. I recognized him, too, but had never met him. Something familiar in his glossy, bloodshot eyes and shaggy hair. I noticed the by-product of a powdery white substance on the table. I knew it didn't belong to us. Clive wouldn't share the remedy without me, not for these tomfools.

Where the fuck is Clive?

I was sure he'd been in the room. I felt his presence. My guess was he came in and interrupted the conversation in order to start his own, just to see if he could, antagonistically imposing his containment of the room for however long he desired. He would do so because no one would have the balls to impede him. Clive carries himself with great confidence, as do I . . . even when we're not confident. We just do it in different ways. Physically we're quite opposite. I'm five nine, thick light-brown hair, blue eyes, lean, aesthetically attractive, and more charming in my demeanor. I'm a good talker that way. Clive—two years my senior—looks more like the spawn of Satan and the Cheshire cat. He's six feet, dark-brown hair shaved close to the scalp (slightly balding), brown eyes, a little heavy, as abrasive as they come, and *that* grin; it made some people afraid to be alone with him. I'm easily liked; Clive is easily feared.

"What's up, guys? Anyone seen my roommate, Clive?" I asked.

"Your roommate?" asked the blonde girl.

"Yeah, Clive . . . Six feet, angry-looking, probably did some of your drugs."

I pointed to the excess cocaine on the table.

The Asian girl whispered something to the blonde and the black guy. They looked up at me like I had a dick growing on my chin. I looked over at the white guy.

"How about you? You seen him?"

"Nope. I haven't seen anyone named Clive come in here . . . What's your name?"

"What's yours?" I asked, taking over the alpha role. "Haven't seen you around here before. You new?"

"Yeah, I'm Reggie's new roommate, Kevin."

There were distinct similarities between Kevin and Kenny Harris—the small eyes, the wiry hair, the drawl in his speech, his size, his build. He looked like a man with greasy secrets, the hidden neighbor who's affectionate toward your puppy until you leave the room. That's when his cards on the table reveal a bluffing hand. He starts to snarl at the innocent pooch. His face contorts to the shape of a lion's growl, reducing his benevolence to a perfidious dust. He kicks the mutt, screams at it, but only when there's no one around. People like that, I want to crucify.

"What happened to what's-her-face from Kansas, the chick who used to live here?" I asked.

"I don't know. Went back to Kansas, I guess. Reggie said she took off about six months ago. Out of the blue, just took off . . . What was your name again?"

I felt a sharp pain in my gut, enough to keel me over. I turned away toward the opposite corner of the room only to be met with painful déjà vu the likes of a rusted knife opening a black hole in my brain. A high-pitched ringing in my right ear stung like a wasp. The volume rose. The pain grew.

"Hey, buddy? You okay?" asked Kevin. "What's your name?"

I saw pictures in my head, bad things. I saw Reggie's roommate, Debbie. I saw Patrick Thornberg crying. I saw myself in the closet mirror, standing over them with the devil in my eyes.

"Hey . . . Buddy . . . What's your name?"

I snapped.

"*Fuck you! That's my name!*"

The ringing stopped. My gut pain receded. I returned to a full upright position. Kevin backed up. Everyone else was frozen. I walked over and rubbed my finger across the excess cocaine on the table in front of him, applied it to my gums.

"You from Texas, Kevin?" I asked.

He was unsteady and confused, sensing the safety had been lifted from a loaded gun. My entire body was a pulse.

"Yeah . . . Houston," he said with a big swallow.

"Thought so."

Kenny Harris was from Texas.

From behind me, a rather low, slow growl crept up the back of my neck.

"Yeah, boy!"

I turned to see Clive waiting in the doorway, his eyes peering down toward Kevin, his posture that of an angered centaur. He looked at me, gave a nod. Clive didn't need to know why I didn't like Kevin. It didn't matter why—that's loyalty. There was no need to cross-examine. We trusted each other in those positions, hunted for answers downstream. I turned and walked toward the doorway where Clive was standing.

"You ready?" I asked.

"Yut," he said, sensing my urge to forsake the bedroom.

Part of me wanted to walk over to Kevin, smash his teeth in with my boot heel. But now was not the time to throw fists— too early for that shit. It wasn't his fault that he looked like an abominable deviant. It would be his fault if he was one. For now, my appetite to do more coke took precedent. I flaked off first, past Clive, who followed closely behind, but not before giving Kevin one more lasting stare.

"That guy reminds me of someone," I said to Clive.

"I know," he said. "But not now."

The voice of reason.

We both, at times, need the other to be the voice of reason, or VOR, as we sometimes refer to it. Mostly, it's me taking on the role of said reasonable voice—about 80 percent of the time. But the other 20 percent, Clive steps in to act as the "situation analysis advocate" for whatever fucked-up state of affairs we've gotten ourselves into—probably by design. That 20 percent staves off potentially epic repercussions. It's an even trade.

We headed back to the living room. I peeked over toward the balcony hoping Niki had cut and run. My malevolence began to evolve into potential violence off the pace of my encounter with Kevin and I preferred she not witness the result of its combustion just yet. She would eventually; they always do.

"She's gone," said Clive.

"Yut," I said.

This is the point in the night where Clive and I felt like the level needed to be raised in order to stay interested. We were growing like weeds in a field of boredom.

"This place is gonna put me to sleep," I said.

"Uh-huh," said Clive.

He pointed to the bathroom on the other side of the apartment. It was vacant. We walked in, closed the door, and locked it.

"Check the cabinet."

"Yut."

We knocked down two lines apiece, drank from the bottle, and commandeered some Klonopin and what was left of the Ambien in the medicine cabinet for the end of the night. I have a hard time sleeping. We stormed out of the bathroom, paid and evil-eyed, crossing the threshold to impending omnipotence, a place where I metamorphize. The structure of my psyche transmutes, and suddenly I become a territorial wretch, like a child hoarding his toys. This tends to happen when I mix cocaine and bourbon with the constant current of anger that swims in my veins—a toxic combination in the district of star-fucking, name-dropping, and false communal togetherness. So many charlatans masquerading in the city of flowers and sunshine can easily set such a person off. One could feel the buildup, the sizzling in the air like power lines. It was going to be another one of those before-dawns where the bootlickers and the blow-jobbers that ended up with Clive and me past a certain hour would either end up stupefied or horrified while sitting front row, forced to witness The Brothers Undignified. I felt invincible. My strengths had multiplied, my fears dematerialized, like I could impel the angels of the lost city to melt into buttered cream by staring intently into their souls. And the night had only just begun. There was so much time to fornicate, fuck up, and forget, comet-tailing a path of bane.

For whom will I exhibit my dark side, demonstrating the way I behold my course and the obscene manner in which I choose to endure it? Who will they be tonight, my believers? Somebody, maybe many, falling in line to form a happy horned coterie of hedonistic little monsters.

But that could have been the drugs talking.

We aimed back toward the balcony with a more intense swagger now. Drowning Pool's "Bodies" exhaled from the speakers like warm breath in a meat locker. Every inch of my body was tense, my jaw was clamped, my teeth were grinding—the dry-fucking of decaying molars like the Earth's plates rubbing together indicating the initial warning signs of seismic activity.

I opened the sliding glass door. To the far left were three girls and two guys, laughing and talking with festive hands. I gave a quick look, noticed a blonde girl. Clive did a double take, racking his brain for some small part of a long-lost memory. He almost looked sad. The blonde looked at us, tightening her pretty, green eyes.

"Who's that?" I asked.

Clive didn't answer. I didn't care enough at the moment to ask again. We leaned against the railing of the vast mezzanine. Clive kept looking at her, the blonde, while I spied the herd inside, pensively thumbing through the predetermined biographies that I'd assumed for them, my jaw still clenched, teeth still grinding.

Out-of-work actor, sullen eyes. Too brooding. Faker . . .

Wannabe, out-of-work actor wearing yellow-tinted lenses and a silk shirt that cost more than that herpes commercial paid him;

doesn't he realize that the three people he's desperately monologuing for want to puke on his shoes?

Actress who's worked her way up from extra to girl-at-the-register in the Burger King commercial. She'll probably end up in porn. Just has that look. I'd fuck her . . .

Guy who came here all by himself and is still standing in the corner all by himself, hands trapped in his pockets. What's he got in there?

Girl who's fucked at least three people here . . . Actually, wait . . . I think I may have fucked her at some point; she looks familiar . . . Yep, make that four. Wait . . . That's the porn girl . . . Aww, shit!

My jaw loosened, reminding me to breathe; the night was young. I inhaled slow and deep, then released. Nobody noticed, but I started to relax. I reached into my tan vintage seventies jacket pocket, pulled out a pack of Camel Wides Lights, and grabbed two smokes. The blonde kept looking over, but I refused to let her know that I noticed, for no good reason. I pulled out a lighter, tilted my head to the left, and, with a snap of my thumb against the spark wheel, ignited a fire at the end of the death stick and inhaled the cancer—a hazardous satisfaction. I gave the cigarette to Clive, then rinsed and repeated. Clive stared at the blonde some more. She was his type. He was a votary of the fair-haired maidens, tall, on the thinner side, and hair about shoulder length—but they were all reasonably disturbed.

"I know her," he said, then drifted off in her direction, left his cigarette on the ground.

"Yeah, man," I said with a tone of indifference, staring into the crowd through the sliding glass.

Our friend, Brandon Tanneker, walked outside. B-Funk, as we sometimes call him, does more cocaine than any two people I have ever met in my life, including Clive and myself. It's astounding that he's still alive. He's a good friend, but he can be work from time to time . . . okay, most of the time . . . okay, every time. Not a midnight proceeds that some poor bastard isn't asking us to take him home because he's talking their ear off, just smashing words together.

"I don't understand what the fuck he's saying."

"He's foreign," we'd say.

Brandon is a close-talking, jaw-wobbling poet who can't formulate a clear word when riding the big white rush. Past a certain hour, it becomes an aneurism-inducing struggle to decipher his wasteful prose through the cocaine-crusted gibberish that impersonates his spoken word. It's ironic that he protests himself a poet. I hadn't seen him in about six months, before Clive's overdose.

"What up, B-Funk?" I said.

Clive noticed Brandon but said nothing. He was too busy clocking Blondie, eavesdropping on her conversation, not engaging. Brandon's eyes were wide as he came in for a hug.

"What up, J-Funk?" he said.

He was coherent, hadn't quite hit his proverbial level yet.

"Just chilling, man. Slaying the age till my show tonight," I said. "What's up with you?"

"Slaying the age. Oh, damn. That's some good shit, Jake. Killing time, right?"

"Right, B. Killing time."

I smiled at him like a father smiles when his child opens a gift that he's been asking for since last Christmas.

"I'm gonna use that one, m'man. You don't mind if I steal it now?"

"Made it just for you, mate."

"Where's the show tonight? Viper?"

"Whisky."

B-Funk looked down at the Jim Beam in my hand.

"No, I'm good."

"I meant the show tonight, dummy. It's at the Whiskey."
He laughed.

"Oh, right. What time?"

"We go on at eleven."

"So, what, like eleven thirty, eleven forty-five?"

"Right."

"You guys been kinda blowin' up lately, huh?"

"Yeah, we're doing okay, I guess. Got some label interest, so . . . I don't know. We'll see."

"Shit. You about to score a deal, huh?"

"That's the plan, but who knows. Tough business."

"Well, you deserve it, man; you guys put on a show. With pipes like yours they better give you something. Man, straight-up rock 'n' roll. They don't have that shit no more."

"Thanks, brother."

Brandon was being kind. I have an unexceptional vocal tone, not classically trained. But I do possess a law-abiding rock-and-roll, bluesy tongue with the faculty to approach the crest of the falsetto from time to time. It's probably more our passion on stage that captivates our subtle but loyal audience, and the songwriting. I cherish floating above the footlights, as hard as it is for me to get up there.

"You been here long?" asked Brandon.

He glanced again toward Clive and the blonde, who were both staring back at him with varied eyes of intent. Clive's face was a shade darker, and his eyebrows were turned down. Blondie's face was a bit scrunched in thought.

"'Bout a half hour. Probably gonna take off soon," I said.

Brandon was still looking in the other direction, sifting through his yesterdays.

"I'll, ahh . . . I'll come check you guys out tonight . . . Eleven, right?" he asked.

"Ish."

"Right."

Brandon leaned in for the exit hug. "Love you, man," he said.

"Love you, too, brother," I said.

Brandon turned to go, then turned back.

"Hey, how you doing with everything, man? I've been meaning to holler at you. You know, with the whole Clive thing? You good? Everything cool?"

I didn't know that B-Funk knew about Clive, about his visit to the hospital. I wasn't sure if he was supposed to know, so I played dumb.

"What Clive thing?"

B-Funk looked at me like I was a child caught lying to his parents about something they wouldn't really be mad about.

"Jake, c'mon, man."

I laughed playfully.

"B, I seriously don't know what you're talking about. Why don't you tell me?"

He looked at me like I was a three-legged dog with my ribs showing.

"Jake . . ." he began. "It's all good, never mind. I'm sorry, man. I didn't mean to bring it up. I just wasn't sure if you, ahh, you know, if, ahh . . ."

"If I what, B? Out with it, man."

"You know what, it's cool, Jake. I gotta take off anyway. We can talk about it another time."

Why doesn't he just come out and say it?

"No, we can talk about it now."

Brandon's phone rang. He flipped it open, waved his finger at me to hold on.

Fuck you, hold on.

"Hey, man, what up? You outside? Yeah, I'll be right down," he said to the voice on the other end, then hung up. Then back to me, "I gotta get outta here, Jake. That's my boy, Roger, downstairs."

"B, what the fuck are you talking about? What thing with Clive?"

He was already halfway across the living room, heading for the front door.

As soon as Brandon left, Clive's voice was in my ear.

"B asking about me?"

"Ahh, yeah, and he's being all weird about it, all secretive and shit. What the fuck was that about?"

"I don't want to get into it right now."

Clive's never said anything like that to me before.

"You fuckin' serious?"

"Later."

"You guys get into some shit or what? He know you OD'd? I didn't want to say anything."

"Sort of . . ."

"And why the fuck is he asking *me* about it? Why is he asking how *I'm* doing? You were right there. He can't just talk to you?"

"Sort of . . ."

"What the fuck do you mean, sort of? You either got into some shit or you didn't. He either knows or he doesn't. Which is it?"

"Later!"

"Oh, top-secret shit, huh? All right, fuck you then."

"Easy, princess. Nothing you can do about it now anyway. C'mon, we've got another party to go to before your show."

"Whatever, Fat Burt Reynolds . . . What party? Where at?"

"La Cienega. Some chick I used to work with at Miyagi's," Clive said as he looked back at Blondie.

There was something lost in his voice. I can't explain it. It just wasn't there. I looked at his watch. Nine thirty.

Plenty of time.

On our way out, Blondie took one more shot at me with her creamy jade eyes. She reminded me of Honey Starskate, a girl who lived across the way from me. Honey has green eyes like that, with dark circles underneath, blond hair, frail, homeless-sexy.

Clive and I started back through the crowd. With no clear aisle, I led us off the beaten path, trampling over the coffee table, leaving a boot-printed crunch across an open bag of potato chips. It sounded like I stepped on a sack of tiny bones, giving birth to a few disapproving glances. Two dipshits sitting on the couch looked up in disgust. They were playing a card game.

"Dude!" said one.

"What the fuck?" said the other.

Clive and I readily turned to engage the fuss. Neither of us took criticism well.

"The fuck is that?" I said. "Dungeons and Dragons?"

Clive said nothing, usually doesn't need to.

They recoiled, quickly reopening a discussion with one another on the topic of who should have won the Oscar for Best Actress in 1999, a typical response from the away team. I understood why, and it has nothing to do with me. I'm not intimidating. Clive, however, with his more bellicose outer shell and brows of hydra, scares the shit out of people.

There were no real threats to us on scene. We knew that the moment we walked into Reggie's. Clive and I are keen to sense those things when, or if, the possibility of an altercation looms overhead. We've befallen a wealth of confrontations where we pissed in someone's cornflakes, enough to salt their cereal. I'd be lying if I said we didn't feast on the violence from time to time. A modern-day joust is a great way to taste your own blood, to remind you that death awaits . . . you know, so you can live. One time, about a year ago, Clive and I brought these two girls to The Cat and Fiddle. It was right after I broke up with Talina.

A LEWD CARNIVAL

"HEY, HOW OLD'S Talina?" Clive asked.

It was a Thursday night. We were pregaming at our apartment, figuring out the night's undoing. Clive was sitting on the couch wearing a cobalt-blue feather boa, camouflage shorts, a short-sleeve Tommy Bahama, and sunglasses on his head. He was rolling a joint to be enjoyed on the other side of midnight while I fingered through a demanding stack of envelopes on the kitchen bar top. The impatiently white rectangles resembled gas bills, electric bills, phone bills.

$180.39—Past Due . . .

$119.27—Past Due . . .

$279.85—Past Due . . .

I contemplated which bill to *not* pay first while my naked toes grabbed at the soft grunge that lay buried deep in the roots of our forest-green shag carpet. Stirring the sulfurous residue of our many guests brought back memories. I didn't mind a touch of grime.

"She's nineteen," I said.

"Pervert," said Clive, tonguing the finishing touch on the joint.

"Fuck you."

"She even got hair on her pussy?"

"No, she doesn't." Clive's eyes perked up as I continued. "I'm not really seeing her anymore."

"Why not? She catch you jerking off to gay porn?"

"I thought you took those videos back," I said while giving Clive the finger. "Actually, she was jealous of you, couldn't handle that your tits were bigger than hers."

"So, what happened? She seemed like she had her shit together—hot, too. You freak her out, try to put it in her butt or something?"

"Did the doctor drop you on your head when you were born?"

"No, I was born in a whorehouse, remember?"

"Did a pimp drop you on your head?" Clive laughed. "I don't know what happened. Just not in the cards, I guess. But she's a good girl, sweet, good heart."

"And you're you . . ."

"Right. And I'm me. I figured I'd eject before the plane crashed."

"But you loved her."

I didn't respond, didn't have to. Clive knows I tend to fall for a girl. Then, when things start to go well, my eyes dilate, my hands begin to shutter, and my legs chatter on life's stage. Then it ends. But I'm not entirely alone in the world. I've got Clive. I'll always have Clive. Just haven't found *her* yet . . .

Talina Yassir was no exception. I wasn't with her very long, three weeks maybe. She was a full-time student, four-point-oh average, majored in public and social service, received modest financial help from her parents. She worked at a coffee shop on the weekends and volunteered at an old-age home two nights a week because she wanted to give back to the community. A real sweetheart, right? And physically she was divine, deliciously Middle Eastern with buttery olive skin crowned perfectly with silky hair the color of burnt sienna. An untarnished innocence searched the outer world for trust through her bright, silencing hazel eyes, and her lips were soft like dough. She was captivating even as she slept. Lying in bed, I'd clock her haunting curves while riding my hand along the whole of her body, slowly ascending, up, up, up, from her calf to her thigh, reaching the midpoint at her hip's crest only to fall fast, dipping down over her oblique and past her rib cage and side breast. She would wake, snapping a breath inward from the tickling of her underarm at the conclusion of my erogenous, fondling roller coaster. My hand would beg to ride again, then my tongue.

We'd only had sex a few times; it was nice enough, fair to middling, mostly because of her inability to feel beautiful, to understand her own allure. She was so nervous to be fully naked without the mask of pitch blackness, where her insecurities could go unnoticed under an armor of darkness. The sex would have been better if she saw herself the way I saw her. She would've had fewer limits. For me, it's difficult to move a relationship forward when the sex is anything but a lewd carnival. If only someone had told her how stunning she was. I tried, but it didn't matter. It was too late. The distorted image she'd had of herself was too deeply rooted, too compacted within her psyche to be dislocated. Dollars to doughnuts, it was planted there by some predatory archfiend she'd been made to trust in the past, in those beginning hours of her emotional development—a piranha disguised as a harmless babysitter perhaps. Or maybe it was just some stupid, misplaced motivational speech that fell from her father's thoughtless tongue, something about how she should spend more time exercising and less time eating. Either way, she was doomed. Trying to change her course now would be like convincing an addict that he doesn't need to choke down copious amounts of cocaine and whiskey just to gut up the fortitude to take the stage. It would be impossible or, at the very least, an Everest-like improbability. Talina is sweet, innocent, a doe, while I'm a meddling rocker, writer, alcoholic, and drug enthusiast who is intentionally navigating the darkness and the dangers of life simply because my team colors are "I don't give a fuck." I didn't want to be held synonymous with her impending disappointment in humanity. So, I walked away, saved myself the embarrassment. That plan was going well for a while.

I changed the subject, didn't feel like talking about Talina anymore.

"Hey, what time are Michelle and her friend coming by? Or are they meeting us at The Cat?" I asked Clive.

"No, they're coming here first. I'm pretty sure Michelle's friend has a boyfriend back East but I don't think that's gonna matter," he said.

"Sweet, what's her name again?"

My indifference to the fact that my date had a boyfriend three thousand miles away couldn't be any more present.

"Chrissy or Christy . . . Hang on."

Clive grabbed his cell phone and dialed.

"Don't ask her what her fucking name is, asshole."

Clive put his finger up to his lips, sarcastically shushing me. I shook my head.

"Hey, what up, sugar pants? What time you guys coming over here? Jake wants to know if he has time to paint his nails."

We flipped each other off in succession.

"Yut, he's so pretty, isn't he?" Clive laughed and continued. "Yut . . . All right. Perfect, bring some booze. Yut! Cool. All right, snookums. Oh, hey, what's your friend's name again? . . . Cool, see you soon."

Clive flipped his phone closed.

"Dick," I said.

"No, her name isn't Dick. Sorry to disappoint. It's Christy, and they'll be here in thirty minutes. You might want to take a shower. You smell like chicken fingers and fuckin' well tequila."

I pulled the bottom of my shirt up to my nose, then released it fast—smelled like it'd been dipped in the fryer.

"Yeah, I better handle that. Gonna take a shower . . . and burn this shirt."

"You got any shirts I can wear tonight?" Clive asked.

"Not unless you wanna sew three of them together, ya fat fuck," I said.

Clive laughed as I shut my door.

Twenty minutes later Christy and Michelle showed up. We pre-partied, had a few vodka SunnyDs, choked down a line—just a taste. Christy ignored the coke, not her thing. The three of them smoked some weed, not me. Marijuana had the ability to render me paranoid so early in the evening. After a half hour of breaking the ice, I had Christy throttled up against the sink between my bathroom and my bedroom. She had an incredible body, a gymnast, solid, still feminine. One scentless candle burned in the dark, creating a pool of smoldering white wax, and a faint beacon the color of a tangerine bounced across the ceiling. The Pixies's "Where Is My Mind?" hissed from the speakers of my thirty-six-inch TV; the hue of its blue screen clung to the music's waves, seeping through the crack in my lair's door, its beryl tone coating our bodies.

Clive and Michelle had quickly accelerated to third base in the living room, adding yet another stain of impurity to the ill-treated sofa. That was only one end of the spectrum for those two opposing psychological misfits. Clive and Michelle have a highly sexual, extremely volatile, especially toxic, on-again-off-again relationship, riddled with fistfights and frying pans that would melt abruptly into barbaric sex infused with a lusty cut of blood drinking and heavy drug use. A wicked game they played—an unhealthy battle of cerebral and bodily malnutrition.

As our kissing intensified, Christy pulled back, stealing the taste of chemical orange from my tongue.

"We shouldn't be doing this. I have a boyfriend," she said.

"Yes, we should," I said.

And so she kept putting her mouth on my mouth; her tongue still touched my tongue. The door to the living room was half-open. Clive was sitting on the couch, pants around his ankles, Michelle's head in his lap, and DMX's "Rough Rider" was on full blast, invading our sound. Christy watched them while I continued to press my lips against her neck. The next kiss was decisive, more her than me. She pulled off her shirt in a single snap, shedding her old skin, ready to be reborn. I kicked the door to the living room shut, then unsnapped her bra. Her stark-white breasts melted into my chest. I grabbed a handful of her long auburn hair with my left hand and tilted her head back, kissing my way down to taste her buttery pink nipples, circling them with my tongue. I spun her around. We were both now facing the mirror, and she pressed her back to my chest. I was rock hard against her ass, rising out of the top of my pants just past my navel. She moaned and I almost ripped out of my skin. I dropped both hands to her waist and undid her pants, pulling down a handful of jeans and panties as far as I could reach. She finished the job for me, legging her way out of the rest. I was still fully clothed. The Doors's "Back Door Man" vibrated from my bedroom with unchaste volume. I turned her around, led her to her knees. She complied, unbuckling my Jack Daniels belt buckle and unzipping my pants. When the warm air hit my Johnny Rocket, it expanded, and Christy took me in her mouth. My pants hung at half-mast, just below my knees. I stopped the action, kicked off my boots, then my pants, then put it back in her mouth. I sailed my shirt up over my head and into the dark; it made no sound, an odd silence. I never did find that shirt. I reached into a drawer on the right by the sink to search for a condom.

I know there's one in here somewhere . . . Not there. Fuck . . .

I checked the left drawer.

Jackpot! Three-pack! Can't read the expiration date . . . Ahh, fuck it.

I ripped open the box, grabbed one rubber safe haven, discarded the rest into the sink. Christy was still taking me in, her cadence causing a welcomed disturbance. I looked down to take in the view. Our eyes met, amplifying the blood flow. I pulled her up and went in for the kiss. I didn't care; it wasn't someone else's dick in there. I spun her back around to face the mirror, ripped open the condom wrapper, and rolled it down to the base. I nudged the inside of her right foot with mine. She spread her legs wider as I grabbed a ponytail's worth of her hair, squeezed just tight enough to induce the slightest erotic pull in her scalp, then led her down toward the sink. She planted her hands up against the mirror.

"Fuck me," she said.

I said nothing.

I entered slowly and started a rhythm, one hand still gripping her hair, the other hand on her hip. Her mouth was open with heavy breath, a high-pitched moan at the end of every gust as I picked up the pace.

Not too fast, don't go too fast.

The mirror told the story. I watched Christy let go of her current life. Such a view to see. Such a thing to know that I could make her forget. And I could watch it all, like I was the star in my own fantastical porn, without the threat of some hacker getting ahold of the video and mailing it back home where Bob the mailman delivers it to Mom with a smile.

"Sign here please, Mrs. Walden."

"What's this?"

"Oh, it's your son's big film debut. You must be so proud. Most people who go to Hollywood overdose and die before they hit it big. Have a nice day."

Christy was dripping with acceptance. I kept driving, going deep. I grabbed her wrists, peeled her palms from the mirror. She pressed her elbows on the countertop. Her breath started to build, heavier, louder. The pitch at the end of her gusts more piercing now. I drove harder, faster, clenching my teeth.

Just a few more seconds . . .

Her body tightened, her eyes went back. I hung on for a few more seconds, then pulled out. She turned to me—I didn't even have to ask—as I snapped the condom off just before the levy broke. Christy dropped to her knees and showed me the way. I exploded into her mouth, tingling from head to toe. My breath slowed. My legs trembled. The heaviness of sweat lagged down the whole of my body like dank Vaseline, slowly pulling me to the ground. We crashed into the beige carpet beneath us, lay there waiting for guilt, like inflamed white chalk outlines at the scene of a murder-suicide. A few minutes later Clive knocked on my door.

"Let's go," he said.

"Yut," I said.

THE CAT AND FIDDLE

THE CAT AND Fiddle was packed as usual on a Thursday night. Clive and I knew the doorman, Long-Hair Johnny, a real skinny motherfucker. He had hair like a hippy, the frame of a junkie, and clothes like rock and roll. I did a bunch of coke with him once, a whole bunch. I won't be doing that again with Johnny. You see, there are certain people who you can party with until the daylight burns, marching to the beat of the Peruvian powder drum, and there are certain people with whom you cannot. I remember Long-Hair Johnny falling noticeably inaudible at the wee hours' delivery, at the tail end of our spirited run, when the sun gored its way in through the fenestra, attempting to illuminate the truth on our stale, ashen faces. Such an honest light revealed Johnny's insecurities because he allowed it to. I always stood strong, denying mine. I am of the steadfast dogma that one must share a deep connection with another in order to maintain a certain level of comfortable un-shitty-ness at the tail end of the white ride. Trust me, what you don't want to see is your copilot shrinking while you're still dashing through the snow—total buzzkill. But he's a nice enough guy.

"Werewolves of London" rendered faintly from The Cat's sound system.

"Johnnaaay, what it look like?" I said as we walked past the long line.

Christy and Michelle trailed behind us.

"Oh, shit," said Johnny.

Clive and I both gave Johnny the man hug.

"Hey, no trouble tonight, you guys," said Johnny with genuine concern.

"C'mon now, Johnny. That shit wasn't our fault," said Clive, referring to the altercation we'd been involved in at the Cat two weeks prior.

The guitar player from some major band was trying to impress upon the girls we were with the current status of his renowned employment, which was fine; the girls were less than galvanized by his pompous braggadocio. But then he started to lay uninvited hands on their asses, so Clive and I punched him and his friends in the face.

"Not your fault? Jake threw the fucking guitar player from the Counting Downs across some poor couple's table . . . *while they were still eating.* And *yooouuu* broke the other guy's fucking nose, asshole. Blood everywhere. What the fuck, guys? The motherfucking Counting Downs."

The Counting Downs had the number-one album in the world at the time.

"Johnny, that band fuckin' sucks. And that curly-haired, wannabe white Lenny Kravitz–lookin' motherfucker was playing grab ass with our lady friends. That guy was crazy in the eyes. He didn't look well."

I turned to Clive.

"That guy looked unhealthy, didn't he?"

"Yut, he didn't look well."

Clive turned to Johnny.

"And homeboy wearing the vest was going after Jake, Johnny. What the fuck was I supposed to do?"

Clive turned back to me.

"That greasy motherfucker wasn't even wearing a shirt under his vest. You believe that shit?"

"Greasy," I said.

"Yeah, yeah, yeah, it's never your fucking fault, guys. But every fucking time you come here, you break something, or someone fucking bleeds," said Johnny.

"Whaaat? Johnny, there's been a few incidents but . . . we're basically like monks when we come here," I said.

"Monks, Johnny," said Clive.

"Oh, really, smart-ass? Monks, huh? Well, let's see here. What about the time that Clive flicked a cigarette in that chick's face? It caused a fifteen-person brawl and we had to close the bar an hour early. Two of my bouncers quit and I came out with a black eye from that shit."

"That bitch owed us a hundred and fifty bucks, Johnny. I confronted her like a gentleman and very gently took her purse. She tried to rip it out of my hands, so . . ." said Clive.

I couldn't help but laugh at the memory.

"Oh, you think that's funny, Jake? I seem to remember a particular happy hour where you got so fucking drunk you whipped your dick out and took a piss in the water fountain."

"You did do that," said Clive.

"Fuck you, sellout," I said to Clive, then turned to Johnny. "Johnny, both bathrooms were closed for cleaning—which is fucking stupid—and besides, nobody even noticed."

"Yeah, Johnny. Nobody noticed his little dick," said Clive.

I punched Clive in the arm.

"It was three o'clock in the afternoon, jackass," said Johnny.

"That's like three incidents, Joh—" I began.

"Then there was the time you initiated a wet T-shirt contest unbeknownst to the girls whose tits you poured your drinks on. The result: angry chicks, angry boyfriends, and more than one fight. Then there was the time you went around stealing food from people's plates thinking that nobody noticed—more fights. Then the time you were blowing lines and smoking opium in the ladies' room. And the time you John-Wayned that guy over the fucking pool table because he was looking at you funny. The time you grabbed a bottle of whiskey from behind the bar and played bartender at some eighteen-year-old girl's birthday party."

"That was all Clive, Johnny. I don't condone that shit," I said.

Clive laughed.

"Hardy fuckin' har. Goddamn animals."

Johnny quickly turned his attention to the ladies behind us, molesting them with his eyes.

"Who's this?" he asked with a wide grin.

Johnny couldn't get girls like Christy and Michelle.

"Take it easy, creeper," said Clive.

"Yeah, don't get weird, Johnny," I said.

Johnny flipped us off.

"Michelle, Christy . . . This is Long-Hair Johnny, the skinniest motherfucker you'll ever meet," said Clive.

"Fuck you, Clive."

The girls said hi.

"Nice to meet you, Michelle and Christy. Mind telling me why a couple of lovely young ladies like yourselves are hanging out with these two asshole degenerate fuckheads?"

The girls laughed.

"I hope you brought your helmets."

The girls laughed some more.

"All right, well, make sure these gentlemen—and I use that term loosely—make sure they behave tonight . . . pretty please."

Johnny put his hands together like he was praying, then opened the gate to let us pass while a small portion of the line grumbled.

"Enjoy," he said.

"Thanks, Johnny," I said.

I passed through the gate, Christy by my side.

"Thanks, brother," said Clive while guiding Michelle.

"Yeah, yeah, I'll be watching you guys."

Clive handed a plastic bag of something to Johnny on his way in.

Finding a table on The Cat's patio would prove to be a long row to hoe at this hour. It was eleven thirty. Oasis's "Wonderwall" was loud. My eyes searched as we trampled toward the restaurant's entrance, past the water fountain, looking for a perch to tranquilize my need to avoid mixing in with the crowd—no such luck. Our consolation was to charge for the bar, check for tables under roof. I was getting thirsty.

No empty tables inside, either. I grabbed Christy's hand and led her through the sea of bodies, drawing back the memory of our intimate brush. She squeezed my hand. Straight to the bar we went, pinching our way through the three-layer line of droughty patrons; they, too, were eager to down the spirits. Mindy Maxine was bartending. Such a pearl she was, buried in a city of shit. A southern girl, down-home pretty with long, light-brown hair always pulled back and kept quiet, tucked inside of her trucker hat atop unblemished skin. She was small in the waist, gray in the eyes, and had strength in her thighs. I didn't know her all that well, but she was always southern sweet to me, fashioned with a kindness and demeanor that only a fool wouldn't want to get to know. As loyal as they come, I'll bet. Not my type, though. Mindy clocked my approach while filling two frosty mugs under the tap. She smiled a whale of a smile, bright white. I nodded back and squeezed between two people to lay elbows on the bar, Christy behind me, Clive and Michelle behind her.

"What are you having, ladies?" I asked.

"Vodka Red Bull," said Michelle.

"I'll have a rum and Coke," said Christy.

I turned to Clive.

"Mate?"

"Bourbon," he said.

Mindy came over.

"Hey, handsome," she said, touching my right hand.

I put my left hand on top of hers and leaned in to kiss her cheek. She smelled like warm biscuits.

"How are you, Mindy?" I asked.

"I'm good, busy as hell, as you can see. What're y'all drinkin'?" she asked with a Tennessee beat.

"One vodka Red Bull, a rum and Coke, and two bourbons . . . Bulleit, please."

"Rocks on the bourbon, right?"

"Yes, please. Both."

"Okay, darlin'. Coming up."

Clive leaned in.

"Gonna go find a table. Meet us outside," he said.

"Yut."

Christy stayed to help bring the drinks. She had fallen mostly inaudible since we left the apartment, stuck in her head, dwelling on the fact that she'd just had me inside of her while her boyfriend waited by the phone.

"Hey," I said. "You're not married, ya know."

The music was loud.

"What?"

I put my lips closer to her ear, felt her eyes close. She tilted her head toward mine, and the sweet smell of apricot danced from her hair to my muzzle. I spoke softly.

"I said . . . you're not married, so have fun. You don't have to figure it all out now."

I pulled away, brushed her hair behind her ear. She smiled back, less genuine.

"Yeah, I guess."

Mindy brought our drinks over.

"Here ya go, honey."

I handed her my credit card with a show of confidence that it would *not* be declined later in the evening.

"Leave it open?"

"Yut. See you soon."

We headed back toward the patio with hope that Clive and Michelle had commandeered a table. I hated standing up all night at the drinkery. I was more of a lounger, a watcher. We contorted our way through the cluster of habitués, trying not to betray our drinks. When we broke the plane of The Cat's threshold, I scanned for Clive and Michelle while "Bad Company" rumbled across the scene.

The Cat was a rather boss establishment. An Old English–style fish-and-chips pub with a lanai twice the size of the rathskeller's innards. The vast outside was bottomed out with cool cobblestone, surrounded by low-hanging trees. I started on the left, clocking the drunkards and half-drunkards. Christy pretended to look, too, but she could see nothing. To the far right I saw Clive and Michelle waving us over. They'd hijacked a winning table in the corner, a little nook, one of my favorite spots, more secluded from the crowd. I could always count on Clive for such things. Four chairs were lined up on the same side of the table, pressing their backs against a wall of flowers, facing the crush. We handed the drinks over to Clive and

Michelle, then sat. I was next to Clive on his left, Christy next to Michelle in the remaining chair to the far right. Clive held his bourbon up to propose a toast.

"Here's to butt sex," he said.

Two of us responded, one didn't.

"To butt sex . . ."

We tipped our glass, tilted back, and gulped the mash. And the songs, they changed.

My favorite part of the night, observing; a preference for thought over conversation. People are always trying to impress one another while pretending not to care. I tend to pull away from the hurry and the harm, to go quiet, holding on tightly to the chair; I breathe better that way. Communicating has always been an effort of necessity—the substance helps.

"What it look like?" said Clive.

"What it is," I said.

"Well, Talina's here."

That was unexpected.

"Where?" I asked as I beat the bushes trying to get a lock on her. "She see you?"

Clive nodded toward the fountain.

"No."

She was at the center of the crowd, all too easy to behold. Christy and Michelle were absorbed with each other; they hadn't caught wind of our conversation, not that it would have mattered. Talina was sitting on the outer crust of the well-spring with her classmate, Melanie—a short, young blonde, semi-cute, nineteen as well; she was more of a rabble-rouser. Clive messed around with her one night. Talina and Melanie were with two six-foot college types, baby-faced Hollywood sons, maybe twenty, stocky, probably played some sort of sport like football or lacrosse. They wore flashy watches, designer sneakers, and name-brand clothes, compliments of their trust funds. Ten bucks says they arrived at The Cat in Junior's BMW 5 Series, payments addressed to Mr. and Mrs. So-and-So What-the-Fuck.

They were all drunk, except Talina. She was hardly an insatiable drinker. The quarterback sitting next to her—let's call him Kip—was trying to impress her with tales of financial never-worry. He wore a trucker hat, tilted to the side, pointed at his watch a lot, made sure she knew how expensive it was.

"Oh, yeah, I see her," I said. "All good."

"All good?" asked Clive.

"Yut."

Clive gave me a long stare.

"All right," he said.

He leaned in to chat with the girls. I looked at Talina. She looked right at me.

Can't look away now.

We spoke without speaking. The eyes don't lie. What did she do wrong? she thought.

I'm sorry.

She missed me.

I'm no good. I did you a favor.

I hadn't formally broken things off with her. I took the coward's way out, gridlocked all communication. She'd dialed a few times, left some messages that went unreturned. Then the calls stopped. That was that.

Talina looked beautiful in her black jeans and lackluster-gray V-neck tee. Kip threw his arm around her aggressively. It pissed me off, but I left it alone, turned my attention back toward present company.

"It's really a pleasurable experience," said Clive.

Michelle laughed. She'd heard it before. Christy did not laugh, and she leered toward Clive an offended look. He was informing the girls, mainly Christy, that RAPE was an acronym that stood for "really a pleasurable experience." Clive has the ability to get under a person's skin, antagonizing a disgruntled response from someone like Christy, who thought he was an abrasive asshole in the first place. It's quite intentional. Those biting quips make it difficult to convince friends that Clive is, indeed, a worthy ally. Most can't fathom why I'm so loyal to him. But they have no idea what it means to be loyal. They're too busy being royal, making it impossible to interpret him the way I do. They sit on the sidelines, smug, sounding off like amateur commentators, branding him a bad seed, the pauper. I try to convince them otherwise, but Clive will usually sabotage it in some way. Doesn't matter, makes me laugh, so many princes and princesses judging from the top floor of their pretentious towers, highfalutin to the hilt. I know that Clive will always be in the trenches with me, that everyone else's hands will remain soft and clean, safe in unblemished white gloves.

Michelle tried to explain Clive's sense of humor to Christy. She didn't get it, then we heard a splash. Talina's friend, Melanie, had fallen into the fountain. Clive laughed hard, louder than anyone on the patio. It drew attention. I laughed, too; who could ignore such an unintentional act of vaudeville? Kip and his friend looked over with bared teeth as they scrambled to help Melanie out of the fountain. Clive and I looked at each other—a recognition at the night's conceivable turn—then back at the bootlickers, acknowledging our willingness to participate in an altercation if they so desired. While Kip's buddy—let's call him Carter—tended to Melanie, Talina and I made eyes. This time we both laughed, shook our heads, and we were together again. Carter noticed; he was embarrassed, irritated. He didn't know any better. Worse, he thought he knew it all. He'd had everything given to him; such a terrible fate. That poor, privileged bastard bumbled over his false sense of the world, using table napkins to mop up his date in a failed attempt at chivalry.

Way to go the extra mile, dipshit.

Kip also noticed the crack in time Talina and I shared. Only *his* upbringing, although similarly privileged, taught him to be more cautious about mad-dogging people he didn't know. He focused more of his attention on Talina. They argued.

None of my business. I'll stay out of it.

The next hour was riddled with key bumps, shots, and Camel Wides Lights. Clive continued to burrow under Christy's skin with his caustic drift while I gave her nothing because I could only think about Talina, whom I tried to avoid staring at but failed. Each time Kip would notice, then Carter would say something to him, and the songs of the night would change again—AC/DC's "Hells Bells" now.

"We need more blow," said Clive.

"Call Bartolo," I said.

As Clive pulled out his phone, I felt a smothering shadow rise over me, a wet blanket dripping at my feet.

"Hey," said a voice.

I looked up, still calm in my chair. Carter was foaming at the mouth, finally built up the courage. He chose me because I wasn't Clive.

"You think that shit was funny?" he asked.

Nothing else was said.

Carter thrust forward and took a swing, a right hand. I saw it coming. He shouldn't have announced his arrival. I leaned back in my chair to dodge the punch. His fist clipped the visor of my Red Sox hat, knocking it to the ground. Before I had a chance to fire back, Clive was on him like angry on a wet cat. He came across the front of me with a whirling right hand. I heard a crunch, sounded like a dog biting into a ceramic skull. Poor, privileged Carter hit the deck hard—lights out.

Kip charged toward Clive, who was hunched over the table in front of us, slightly off-balance from the force of his punch. I came out of my seat like a champagne cork, over the top of Clive with a straight right hand. Kip's nose exploded, a burst of bright red. It was like punching an egg full of blood. There were a few faint-hearted screams and Kip folded like a lawn chair. We hadn't noticed the third guy. He must have arrived after the shit hit the fan; Spencer, we'll call him, a larger fellow, longer. Long-Hair Johnny and two burly henchmen were charging toward us.

"*Break it up, guys!*" yelled Johnny.

Spencer came in like a windmill. Clive and I went straight for him. I got hit on the way in, just a glance off the top of my head—nothing doing, my hair was already a mess. It quickly turned into a yarned ball of arms, fingers, and fabric as Johnny and company melted into the fracas. Spencer got ahold of Clive's ugly Hawaiian shirt, tore it down the front before the bouncers subdued him; he was still fighting to break their hold when Johnny stepped in front of Clive.

"Those motherfuckers started it, Johnny," said Clive.

Spencer broke free and went for Clive, who didn't see him coming. No matter, I did. I intercepted with a cold right hand. He never saw it, got him flush on the temple, knocking him back into the bouncer's arms. My hand ballooned. He took the punch better than his friends, didn't go to sleep. Clive tossed Johnny to the side and went for Spencer. I grabbed Clive, got his eyes to see my eyes.

"We're done," I said.

"Get these guys out of here," said Johnny to the bouncers, referring to Kip, Carter, and Spencer.

Two other bouncers came over to assist, picked Kip and Carter—still rubber-legged—up off the ground, and escorted them to the front. A half-moon of patrons was staring at

Clive and me. I saw Talina talking to the bouncers. They were motioning for her and Melanie to leave as well. She looked at me the way a sad story ends. I was stark naked, unambiguous, my true colors colliding with the night, casting a shadow that hung like the nature of violence. She saw the side of me that I never wanted her to see. But what choice did I have? And what choice did she?

"You good?" asked Clive.

"Yeah, you?" I asked in return.

He was fine. Johnny looked pissed.

"What the fuck, guys?"

"Sorry, Johnny," said Clive.

"Yeah, sorry, Johnny," I said.

"You saw those guys started it, though. Asshole threw a punch at Jake."

"Every fucking time you come here I gotta throw somebody else out. Every. Fucking. Time."

Clive and I stood there like bad children. Johnny shook his head, breathing heavily from the rush.

"Man . . . you guys . . ."

"No more violence tonight, Johnny, I swear. Let's have a shot," I said.

"C'mon, Johnny. On us," said Clive.

Johnny started to smile, still trying to catch his breath. He loved the action, to tell you the truth. Clive and I had been in so many fights on his watch. It was usually the most exciting part of his night. A waitress walked by. Clive got her attention. She was older, leather skin, smoker's voice, had held a lifetime of drink trays.

"What can I get for you boys?" she asked, then looked at Johnny. "You okay, Johnny? You look tired."

"I'm fine, Marie. Bring us a couple shots, would ya?"

"What do you guys want?"

"Tequila," said Clive.

I nodded.

"Tequila," said Johnny.

"How many?"

Johnny looked at us. We looked at the girls; they were still in shock from the evening's mad release.

"You girls want a shot?" I asked.

"Ahhh . . . yeah, that was crazy. I definitely want a shot," said Michelle.

Christy didn't say anything, just nodded in agreement. Something had once again chased her past away.

"Five shots of Patron," said Johnny. "And can you grab a Cat T-shirt for this asshole, please?" he continued, pointing to Clive. "Put the shots on my tab, though."

Johnny turned to Clive.

"You guys are fucking paying for the shirt."

Johnny turned back toward Marie.

"Go ahead and give 'em my discount on the shirt."

"You got it, Johnny. Coming up."

Marie turned toward Clive.

"What size, honey?"

"What's the biggest one you've got?" I asked.

"Fuck you, dick," said Clive, then turned to Marie. "Extra large is fine, thanks."

"And can you bring a bucket of ice, too, please?" I said as Clive and I held up our war hands.

"Ouch. Sure thing, honey."

She came back with the shots, the ice, and a black Cat and Fiddle T-shirt. Christy was sitting on my lap as was Michelle on Clive's. Johnny and two bouncers were sitting next to us talking and laughing about the fisticuffs. I kindly pulled Marie the waitress down to me, motioned toward the T-shirt, and whispered in her ear.

"Put that on my tab, please."

"What's the name?"

"Walden. First name's Jake."

As Oingo Boingo's "Just Another Day" careened off the cobblestone, we held our glasses high.

"*Salud!*"

And all eyes went to the sky.

SNOWBLIND

AFTER THE CAT and Fiddle we took a Yellow Cab back to Yucca. Bartolo was waiting out front, across the street.

"Let's go, ladies," I said to Christy and Michelle.

I nodded to Clive.

"Be right up," he said.

Christy and Michelle followed me into the apartment building while Clive walked across the street to do business. I gave Bartolo a halfhearted wave. His response was to roll up his half-rolled-down window.

Nice to see you, too, Bartolo.

I opened the front door.

"After you, ladies," I said, not taking my eyes off Clive.

I'd always felt ill at ease, just a trace, whenever Clive got into Bartolo's car, lost to view behind the cold, black tint of instability—Bartolo was *not* our friend. The car drove off. The girls and I went upstairs. Christy and Michelle went for the couch. I went for the fridge, pulled out the vodka, SunnyD, and red Gatorade—Yucca cocktails. I opened one of the cabinets, grabbed two coffee cups—both covered in dust—a red keg cup turned upside down, and a single highball glass.

That'll do.

Everything else we owned by way of china was in the dishwasher, bathing in its own filth. I rinsed the coffee cups and rigged the liquor. Michelle sipped hers. Christy put hers down. I went to the patio for a smoke while the girls covered the sofa with conversation, recap of the night. It was, after all, an eventful evening. Clive came in and headed straight for the balcony.

"What were *you* doing out there?" Christy asked as if she knew him better than she did.

Clive ignored her. Michelle leaned in to tell her he bought some cocaine.

"We good?" I asked.

I took a drag, rubbed my hands together in excitement. And there was that grin.

"Ya, boy," said Clive, holding up a bag full of white rocks.

"What the fuck is that?"

"Rock . . . You smoke it."

"Yeah, I know that, dickhead. What happened to the powder?"

"He didn't have any. But if you like snorting it, you're gonna love smoking it."

"Yeah?"

"Trust me. It'll ring your bell."

"Ring my bell?"

"Yeah, that was wicked stupid."

"Fag."

For five whole seconds I felt smug, high above the act. Then my eyes went afire and a flood of excitement—enough to fill the Grand Canyon—curled around my insides, wreaking candor. We are who we are. Over Clive's right shoulder I noticed Christy making her way to my room. She looked at me to see if I'd noticed. She wanted to fuck. I wanted to smoke cocaine.

"Fuck it, I'm in. I'll be right there. Don't start without me," I said to Clive as I walked past him.

"Hurry up. Max and Bill are bringing some people by to party," he said.

Max Mason and Bill Bellows were good friends, worked with us at the Lux. I followed Christy to my bedroom. Michelle was up off the couch and in the wind to join Clive on the patio. I opened the first door. Off to the right wept a leaky faucet, a slow drip. Christy's handprints were still on the mirror. I noticed a familiar blue light seeping through the crack of my bedroom door. I opened it. Christy was sitting on my bed wearing only a white V-neck T-shirt and red panties—the T-shirt was mine. The rest of her clothes were on the floor at the foot of the bed. She was leaning back on her hands, her legs slightly open, her toned thighs luring me. I was getting hard.

"I was gonna put some music on, but I didn't know how to work it," she said.

"What do you want to hear?"

"Whatever . . . Or *you* could play something for me."

I pretended I didn't hear her, grabbed the CD case on top of my copy of Hemingway's *The Sun Also Rises* that rested on the blue milk-crate end table next to my bed. Christy bit her lip at the presence of my flyby, rubbed her leg against mine like a cat that wants you to know you're part of their circle. I grabbed the first disc, Black Sabbath *Vol. 4*, put it in the DVD player, and hit the *RANDOM* button. Track six, "Snowblind," began; it was too loud. I sedated it, down to a low hum.

"Come here," she said.

I knelt down to her level, my hard-on pressing against my bed. She gave me her lips, still a subtle taste of chemical orange from the SunnyD. She was a good kisser, went at a good pace, didn't overuse her tongue; it was effective. I wondered if Michelle was going to smoke with us. I knew she was into blow, but I didn't know if she'd be the type to smoke it—smoking cocaine comes with an uglier mask, puts you in a greasier club.

Christy came off as a prude; she'd be appalled, but I didn't care. Either she was going to wait for me in my bed, which was the perfect scenario—wired now, naked later—or she was going to judge me while I smoked drugs. I felt the urge to hurry.

"Hey, why don't we go hang out for a bit first," I said.

"I'm done drinking," she said. "Stay here with me. I want you to fuck me again."

She was a bit sloppy, but her words still made my pants pop. A woman who speaks bluntly, sexually—it always drives me nuts.

"Tonight was exciting," she said.

I was surprised she admitted to such a thing.

"Let's just hang out for a bit first, just a little while. Then we can fuck," I said.

She went in for another kiss. I accepted and her body weakened. Then she spoke again.

"Let's fuck now."

She grabbed my cock over my pants.

The tip-top of my tenacious D was stabbing my left inner thigh, trying to pry its way out of my jeans. I brushed her hand away and forced my hard-on back down to the side, trying to murder it in my trousers. It felt like it was going to snap.

"Soon," I said. "I wanna hang out for a bit first."

"To do drugs?" she asked.

"Yeah, but I wanna hang out, too. We've got some friends coming by."

"I'm not really into those kinds of drugs, though. I've never done coke before, not really my thing."

"You don't have to do any. Just come hang out."

"I'd rather just hang out with you, in here."

This is taking too long.

I pushed some dangling strands of hair back behind her left ear.

"I'll tell you what . . ."

I kissed her lips.

"You lie down for a bit . . ."

I kissed her neck.

"I'll go hang out for a little while, for like an hour . . ."

Back to the lips.

"Then, I'll come back . . ."

I knew damn well that I wouldn't be back in an hour, but I was trying to close the deal.

Always be closing!

I called to mind my sales team leader from Hooked on Phonics. He'd vomit the overused dictum to us on a daily basis during our grossly enthusiastic morning pump-up. I worked there for about six months, right before I migrated to Hollywood from Orange County.

Christy moaned with reluctance, then caved, agreeing to my selfish plan.

"Okay, but don't be long," she said.

"I won't be," I said, staring a thousand leagues into her eyes, to where the drugs were. "I promise."

My dick was still raging, contra to what it would be like for the next four or five hours. But my thirst to get high was greater than the girth of my innate lust. I tucked my throbbing appendage as far down as it would go while Christy curled under my navy-blue comforter, certain of my return. As I walked out of the room, my excitement hit DEFCON 1.

One might think that to be odd, having just abandoned a beautiful woman who lay half-naked and randy in my bunk. I had declined sex in order to smoke cocaine. This was a whole new gutter.

When did I start making these kinds of decisions?

There was a time when bedding a hot girl—even the possibility of having sex with her—took precedent over anything and everything, but now, all I could think about was: *What will it feel like? How long will it last? What will it taste like? Will I get that drip in the back of my throat like when you snort it? Will I get that same rush, or better? If it's anything like the powder, then everybody will love one other and everything will be extraordinary . . . and I won't want it to end.*

Michelle was passed out on the couch in the living room, her jacket covering her. Clive's bedroom door was open.

"What up, boy?" he said as I walked in.

"So, how do we smoke this stuff?" I asked.

On his end table topped with a square slab of clear plastic lay four rocks in a small copper bowl. He held up a glass pipe and put the rock inside at the top.

"Hold it pointing up when you first light it. When it starts to burn, turn it down and inhale slowly. If you go too fast you'll burn your throat," he said.

I grabbed the lighter and held the pipe to the sky.

"Let's get high," I said, closing the door behind me.

Oh, wow . . . Wow!

I've never felt anything so satisfying in my life. And I never went back into my room that night.

I was still awake at first light—something I was hoping to avoid—out on the balcony suffering through a half-smoked cigarette that I'd plucked from an overflowing ashtray. The morning was silent. Still, I wore sunglasses to protect me from any potential human contact. Bill was crashed on the couch, covered from head to toe in a raggedy light-brown comforter, trying to avoid the apocalypse of sunup—he'd freebased as well. Michelle was with Clive in his room and Christy was alone in my bed. I sat in the lonely quiet of a sad new day, getting ready for the crash, always the dreadful reward of flying around the vault of heaven at night on the pale horse, straight into daylight. This was a particularly difficult crash because I'd just smoked cocaine for the first time and left a beautiful girl waiting in my bed. I didn't feel great about myself, but I knew that I would do it again.

Christy came out of my room. She looked at me through the sliding glass door for longer than a moment. Thank God the slider was closed. She was tired, embarrassed, regretful, disappointed. I was sad because that's what it feels like when you come down. And that's what it feels like when someone tells you they wished they'd never met you with just a look. Christy left. I went to my room, shut the door, pinned two black bedsheets across my window to kill the sun, and curled up in a ball in my bed, avoiding everything, avoiding everyone, fighting back the tear-jerking realities of my life. I couldn't sleep. I tried to get off, watch a movie, tried to read *Fear and Loathing in Las Vegas*. I picked up my guitar, couldn't play. I tried to not think about the night before but to no avail. I didn't dare open the curtains to be judged, fearing that someone would recognize that a part of my face had melted off.

What's happening to me?

I never saw Christy again. I was relieved at that.

9:35 PM – AUGUST 13

CLIVE AND I started out of Reggie's in pursuit of more drugs at Tricia's party, the girl he said he knew from Miyagi's. I looked around for Reggie before we left, felt the need to ask about his old roommate, Debbie, from Kansas. I was curious as to the circumstances of her abrupt departure.

Must be in his room. Fuck it.

We left, slip-sliding on the human stains. I called a cab as soon as we hit the hallway.

"Cab will be in here in twenty. Gotta take a piss," I said to Clive.

We headed back to our apartment.

When I came out of the bathroom, Clive was nowhere in sight. His door was closed.

I walked out to the balcony for a smoke, flashing across the way. I looked at Honey's window; she wasn't there. The curtains were drawn.

I'll catch her in the morning.

Honey Starskate was a season ticket holder in the break of my day, always an apocalyptic vibe, like everyone else in the world had died. She moved in six months ago when Clive was out of commission, ended up on Yucca after Vegas left her high and dry. Clive's never met her. We chat sometimes in the mornings when Clive is still asleep, sitting on our sills enjoying a smoke, both sad and dreaming about tomorrow, trying to lay waste to the imperfections of our yesterdays. I'd get out of bed having most likely struggled to sleep, sporting my ritual raging hard-on. I'd hit the can to have a piss, hunched over, practically upside down, hands to the floor to keep from falling on my face, save staining the walls a dark, liquored yellow—a residual discharge compliments of the night before. After my thirteen-minute upside-down piss, I'd go back to bed to resuscitate my now half-flaccid dong for a morning jerk.

Who'll it be this morning?

Following a twenty-minute struggle to release my army of Satans into a nearby sock or boxer briefs, I'd head to the kitchen to brew a pot of coffee—whatever we'd stolen from the restaurant that week. Then I'd spark a Camel, crack a window, drag the gasper, and, with luck, find myself face-to-face with one of the most interesting people I'd ever met. Honey was a good listener, agreed with me plenty, and for twenty minutes or so I'd forget about any pain. Then the birds would chirp and she'd have to go, and real life would take her place. She was a bit older than I was, kind of like a big sister, the one I never had. She was trying to break into the porn industry—talk about a vile business. Anyway, she wasn't home, so I looked up at my old apartment, where I lived with Peter and Little Ben.

SEVEN AND SEVEN

I MET PETER and Ray Zimmerman and Little Ben on the Fourth of July in 1997 at Randy Rabaduski's house in Newport Beach. Randy I knew through my roommate, Jimmy (Jimmy Nuts, I called him). Jimmy's an old friend from back East who let me crash at his pad when I first moved out to California. He's a former marine turned entrepreneur, always looking for a way to make a buck.

Jimmy and I turned down 34th Street, found a spot in front of Randy's. I clocked the big-nosed Romanian strolling on the patio, snapping his fingers, smoking a Cohiba. The bright orange end of the cigar burnished phosphorescent with every draw while "Luck Be a Lady" spit class into the air like mist from a broken wave. It was eighty-five degrees and sunny, the entire sky a canvas of powder blue—not one cloud. Jimmy and I got out of the car.

"Whataya say, fellas?" said Randy.

"What's up, devil dog?" said Jimmy.

"Rab-a-doo," I said.

Everything seemed routine for Newport Beach, the neighborhood a cluster, houses practically stuck together like the ivory keys of an old grand, one resembling the next if not just for its mediocre condition. It was quiet now, but in a few hours the streets would be packed, full of drunk twentysomethings looking for kicks in the sandier version of Beverly Hills. Most of the renters were paper college students with wealthy parents. Mommy spent most of her time at Fashion Square Mall buying black dresses and Gucci bags while Daddy—the stuck-up, immoderately proper dick fart and demented partier—would relish in the warm, wet hug of his secretary's lips wrapped around his cock as he made stock positions in order to support a massive coke habit. At noon he'd call it a day, dog his $250,000 Mercedes Benz over to the dock—drunk and wired—to meet his girlfriend on his even more expensive ninety-two-foot Beneteau. Out for a winter's sail they'd go. Then there were the mentally nonexistent surfers who loved to get strobed and whipped by the curl . . . or whatever. They were living the dream but unable to pay for it. The girls had a Hollywood attitude and the integrity to match. Receiving absurdly large amounts of money from their Fortune 500 CEO daddies on the reg will do that to a person. In some cases, it was their *actual* father.

Jimmy popped the trunk. We grabbed two grocery bags, a bottle of Beam, and a thirty-pack of Coors Light. With one deep breath, I thought of only the bounding main—an autogenetic response for me anytime my nose caught wind of the brine and my ears netted the sultry command of the deep, beautiful monster with frosted white tips. It reminded me of summers in Gloucester, writing songs near the waves. I gave a nod to Wes and Jared (Randy's roommates), hugged Randy, then announced my withdrawal. I put the beer and the Beam down, cracked open a Coors Light, and followed the salty trace. I stepped out of my flip-flops when the concrete collided with the sand, continued to where the dry sand and the wet sand overlapped. I sat, and my eyes swept the never-ending drink, which filled them to a wet swell from the cool air that ran across the ocean's surface and into my face. I just wanted to look at her, feel insignificant, happy and sad. The ocean could kill me if it wanted to. I admired that.

I wiped the moisture from my eyes and walked back to the house. Jared and Wes were chatting it up with Jimmy—Wes used to live with Jimmy. Randy walked outside, Seven and Seven in hand, Sinatra's "The Lady Is a Tramp" echoing the length of the street like it was a cavern.

"Cheers, fuckers," he said.

I grabbed Randy for another hug. He's a lovable guy.

"Thanks for having us, brother," I said.

"My pleasure."

"Early start on the stogies, eh?"

"You know how I do when Sinatra's in town."

"Good ole Frankie."

"My boys will be here in about ten minutes. You're gonna love these guys."

"So you've said."

He probably said the same thing to *them* about *me*, a generous accreditation. As I was torturing myself about living up to expectations, two girls pedaled by on their cruisers, both blond and petite, tan with black bikinis and flawless bodies, ripe at the age of twenty, twenty-one. I grabbed another beer. One girl rode a turquoise bike, the other, pink. I tipped my beer to Pink. She smiled.

"Happy Fourth, ladies," said Randy.

"We're having a little get-together here later. You should stop by," said Jimmy.

"Sure," they said.

Turquoise recognized Wes. He was tall and blonde, looked like a surfer instead of a punter for the Minnesota Vikings, a job for which he had recently lost his contract.

"Hey, you know my roommate, Melissa, right?" she asked him.

Wes stared like a dunce.

"Oh, yeah . . . Melissa . . . Yeah, I know her," said Wes.

I looked at Pink. She wasn't buying it. We both smiled about it.

"What are your names?" I asked.

"I'm Jen, this is Tammy," said Pink.

"I'm Jake, this is Randy, that's Jimmy Nuts, you know Wes, and that's Jared . . . Say hi, Jared."

Jared clenched his lips together, cheek bones rising in a toothless half smile. He always thought his girlfriend was spying on him.

"Maybe we'll see you later then," said Jen.

A light blue 1976 BMW 2002 pulled up, Quiet Riot's "Come On Feel the Noise" bouncing off the steaming granite. They parked across the street, a few houses down. Peter, Ray, and Little Ben got out.

"What's up, fellas?" said Randy.

The girls said they'd stop by, got back on their bikes, and pedaled toward the beach. Jen looked back. I gave her a smile, then forgot about her. I was sure I'd run into some version of her later in the evening. Four houses down, the girls stopped again—more hopeful admirers.

Peter was the younger of the two brothers by two years. He was tall, six foot two, handsome in a White House errand boy sort of way. He had on blue cargo shorts and a red polo with the collar down—trying to capture the spirit of the holiday, I guess. He looked like one of those yacht club douche-baggingtons whose self-indulgence is matched only by the epicurean desires of a rich politician. If he had his collar up, I'da punched him in the dick. Ray—big brother—was not quite as tall, maybe five eleven, movie-star looks, big head, movie-star gait. He had on mirrored Top Gun aviators, army-green cutoff shorts, and a black Metallica T-shirt. Now we've got the good-looking older brother who thinks he's an artist because he goes on auditions and owns a guitar. Ben was a childhood friend of the brothers. He was five foot three with no room to hedge, wore a Redskins hat, board shorts, and a faded gray *Dukes of Hazzard* shirt, looked like Marty McFly. I judged them out of fear that they would be judging me, I, with my Red Sox hat on backward and cutoff sleeves looking like the drummer in some wannabe Blink 182 band.

To this point Randy had done such a bang-up job of hyping everyone up to one another that the initial handshake was nerve-racking. The way he talked about these guys you'd think the curtain would fall, and suddenly we'd find out that *their* father had fucked *my* mother on some business trip, knocked her up, and out I popped nine months later—long-lost brothers meeting for the first time.

We exchanged standard pleasantries, then—I can't remember who started it—the four of us began rifling off movie lines, flawlessly intertwining them within the conversation. We were all buffs. Laughter ensued, and that immediate comfort of camaraderie set in like the clouds of a wanted storm. It was impossible not to like them. Jimmy and Randy were lost but still laughed, because they knew how it would go. They told me so.

I tended bar in the kitchen, made Seven and Sevens. Randy and Jimmy smoked cigars on the patio, watching a composite of bikini-clad stunners fill the streets. Jared and Wes played Kings, Sinatra sang, and we all drank plenty, chatted about random things. Inside, Ray told a joke—something about a horse cock. Just as Ben walked past, I spat a bulbous gulp of colorless soda and blended American whiskey in his face. While I choked on the comedy, he smiled and froze, eyes still closed, taking one for the team in complete silence as the bubbly drip-drop dribbled down his face and hung from his chin. Reactions fell like a trail of dominos. Peter's drink bled through his nose, his face distorting like a Picasso, convulsing in a silent, painful laugh. Ray tumbled backward over the arm of the couch. The slap of his open palm hitting the white tile floor was barely audible as we all lost our guts from the pulse of laughter.

The drinking continued into the night. We stopped at a few houses, a few bars, inviting every girl we met back to Randy's for after hours. We ended up at an Irish pub, Malarkey's. I felt good, elated, that moment of the high and the night that shields you from all that is wrong with yourself. Ray and I were chatting up two women, a tall blonde named Sarah and a saucy five-foot *chiquita* with more tattoos than bare skin named Ez. Sarah was drunk on Ray, her hands all over him. She was blatant without burden because he made her laugh and he was handsome. Ez played it a bit tougher with me, except when I made *her* laugh. She sipped tequila. Peter and Ben were at the bar working a couple potentials. The place was small, the music was loud, and nothing bad had happened.

"You girls should come back with us," said Ray.

"Okay," said Sarah.

Then a portion of the crowd to the right opened like a small wound. Some beach-haired bro wearing barely a tank top bled through, bumping Ray, pulling Sarah aside.

"What the fuck are you doing?" he asked her.

"Trevor, stop," she said.

Ez slammed her tequila. Ray was about to move in. Trevor noticed and turned, chest pressed out to make sure we knew he had one. I stepped in before the next sound was made. It only takes a few seconds, one look into someone's eyes to know who they are in situations like this. I haven't won every fight I've ever been in, but I always know which ones I'm going to win and which ones might not go my way. But when it came to defending a friend, none of that mattered. Staring twelve inches up at Trevor, I knew how this would go. I wanted to light his face up with the color of my ire. It was moments like this that induced its birth. My hands ejected right through the low part of his chest in a short burst, sending him backward a few feet. His eyes marveled at such bold aggression from someone giving up fifty pounds. Only a few patrons noticed, not enough to raise the hairs on any of the bouncers yet. Trevor shivered like a child and his face turned the color of a beet. He looked over at Sarah. She was embarrassed for him. He had to do something to prove he was a man.

"What the fuck, dude?" he said.

Way to dig into the platitudes, ass-face.

In a desperate attempt to prove himself, he raised one hand to my shoulder—rather apprehensively—and tried to shove me back. I recalled something my dad said when I was nine years old. He said, "Hit 'em square in the nose, and not only will it bleed, but his eyes will water, and he won't be able to see. Then you either got him or you can run." So, I punched him in the nose. Trevor's nose bled, his eyes watered, and he crumpled to the floor, laid out in stale beer.

Sarah ran over to check on him while Ez stood near the scene with a sinister smile, a sexy one. Peter and Ben rushed over to see what the fuss was when the bouncers moved in. Ray and I held our hands up as if we had nothing to do with it as the bouncers moved past us and tended to Trevor.

"What the fuck happened?" asked Peter.

"Ask Rocky," said Ray, motioning toward me.

"Explain later. Let's go," I said.

Outside, Ray explained the incident with pride. Peter was especially grateful knowing someone else would stick up for his brother the way he would have. He and Ray were close, like brothers should be, and their appreciation was twenty-four carat.

A few hours later, I ran into a familiar face on some rooftop party a few streets over from Randy's. Shandra. I'd messed around with her a couple weeks prior on a hiking trip up in Big Bear that Jimmy Nuts and I had taken. It was random to see her, but nice. Her skin was a buttery-smooth, dark-chocolate brown, and her breath was especially minty, like it was in Big Bear. Heavy groping ensued. We saw Sarah and Ez at the same party, no Trevor. Sarah pounced on Ray, but Ez gave me nothing. No matter, I had Shandra. As the party died down, we all went back to Randy's. A dozen girls or so followed, and a few dudes that Randy knew.

Seven and Sevens were poured. Stogies burned orange in the night. What a time it was. Ben disappeared to the back bedroom with a girl much taller than him. Peter was alone, but on the hunt. Shandra and I decided to escape the collage of drunken conversations, falling victim to the sound and scent of the sea, the curtain of Cimmerian shade slowly revealing itself the more our eyes adjusted to the dark of the night. We fell to the cold, wet sand just a few feet from the water, kissing, undressing. We danced our way into the deep, struggling to balance as one in the thrust of the curl. The moment there was a break in the current I entered her; she rested buoyant with her arms wrapped around my neck, her eyes to the stars as I tried to hold a steady measure. It was difficult to maintain balance. But such a flight of fancy under the moonlit sky was not something to discontinue, so when the current reestablished its dominance, I walked her up to the dry sand, her goose-pimpled legs still straddling me, gripping me for leverage. We fell into the cotton earth, pulsed in tempo until our bodies stretched long and quivered.

We dressed, then headed back to Randy's, invariably detached for the remainder of the evening. Later on, Peter and Shandra found themselves alone in the corner, locked in conversation. He had no idea what had occurred on the beach. Then, I found Ez.

The next morning I walked out of the back bedroom. Ez was still asleep. We stayed up pretty late. She had cocaine, let me do some off her ass. She was dangerous sexy, even first thing in the morning, mouth wide open, bed-headed and half-naked. Ben and the giant girl he was with had slept on the floor in the same room—her feet were sticking out of the blankets.

When I came out to the living room, Jimmy and Randy were already awake and making coffee, whistling something. The front door was open, revealing another warm summer day. Ray and Sarah were sitting in a rattan in the corner, still romanced with each other. Peter was still asleep on the couch, spooning Shandra. I couldn't resist—I told everyone what had happened between Shandra and me before she and Peter woke.

Shandra skedaddled as quickly as she could put her shoes on, indifferent to the night's affairs. She was a bit of a gypsy. After she left, Peter informed us of his valiant but failed efforts to get into her pants.

"Fuck, man, I ended up cuddling with her all night," he said.

"No go, huh?" I asked.

"Nothing . . . and she was fucking covered in sand. I've got sand in my ass, in my mouth . . ."

"Umm . . . why do you have sand in your ass?" asked Ray.

Everyone laughed.

"She's a nice girl. Jimmy Nuts and I met her up in Big Bear last month," I said.

"Jake, weren't you hanging out with her last night? Didn't you guys go down to the beach?" Jimmy asked, playing along.

"Oh, shit, that's right." I paused, winked at Peter, smiled like I just took all his money in a card game. "Sorry about the sand, Peter."

His smile and his eyes grew as he looked around the room.

"You fucked her, didn't you?"

Laughter ensued.

"I did, yes. I did fuck her . . . and apparently you cuddled with her afterward . . . so . . . thanks for that."

The laughter continued.

Randy and Jimmy Nuts were right, I loved those guys. Two weeks later I moved up to Hollywood to live with Peter and Little Ben on Yucca, slept on the couch in the living room. Making it big in Hollywood was always my intention, to be a rock star. And that's where I met Clive, on Yucca.

CLIVE SALTON

I WAS LINGERING on the balcony of my two-bedroom dump—an overcast day—smoking a Camel, drinking a Natty Light with my roommates, Peter and Little Ben, and Peter's brother, Ray, who lived up the street. I spent a significant amount of time out there on the balustrade, often trying to recollect the last time I'd checked the nasty little crevices of our abode for loose change—enough to purchase a cheap twelve-pack of some shitty pilsner. I'd liberated myself from the annoyance of having a job for over a month now, since leaving behind my sales job in Orange County. I was mostly fine with it, until I ran out of cash. Eventually I had to pick up some part-time work doing craft service. Mom sent a little money, but that wellspring, I could tell, was receding. My roommates weren't consistently employed at the time, either—once in a while, Peter and Ray would bartend an event at the Palladium, pocketing enough cash to last a month or two. Ben did promotional stuff, some PA work on and off. We all had plenty of time to kill, so we sharpened our knowledge of movies from the eighties and nineties while competing in concentrated games of Caps—throw a bottle cap into your opponent's cup, if you sink it they drink it.

Peter, Ray, and Ben stepped inside as our delivery from Big Wang's arrived. I stayed outside to finish my smoke and play the guitar. Clive came out of his apartment, scanning the empty space on his balcony. He was wearing jeans and a Red Sox hat on backward, no shirt. He was thinner then. I could see cardboard boxes through the sliding glass door, scattered in the living room. Clive lit up a smoke, closed his eyes, and inhaled; he was smiling. When he opened his eyes, he saw me across the way.

"What it look like?" he said.

It was my first introduction to his distinct, low, gravelly tone; it fit him perfectly.

"What it is," I said.

"I'm Clive."

"I'm Jake."

"Nice to meet you, Jake."

"Nice to meet you, too, Clive."

He took another drag while I did the same. I finished the rest of my beer, put my guitar down.

"What was that you were playing? Sounded good," he said.

"Aw, it was nothing much. Song I was working on."

"Song about a girl, yeah?"

"Yeah, sure."

We both recognized the cliché.

"Where you coming from?" I asked.

"Maine," he said.

"I'm from Boston."

"Yah, boy."

"So what brought you out here?"

"I didn't want to go to jail."

"For what?"

"Assaulting farm animals," he said with a grin. I laughed. He continued, "I'm an actor."

"Cool."

"You out here for music?"

"Yut."

His roommate, Samuel, came out on the balcony wearing scrubs and handed Clive a Guinness.

"Let's do some fuckin' drugs tonight. I've been pinching pills off the top at work for the past month," said Samuel to Clive.

"What did we get?"

"Everything."

"Yah, boy," Clive said, then turned to me. "Hey, this is my roommate, Samuel . . . Samuel, that's Jake."

"Nice to meet you, Jake."

"You, too, Samuel."

Samuel went back inside to unpack more boxes.

"I think we're gonna get fucked up tonight. You and your roommates come on by," said Clive.

"Yeah, maybe we'll stop by," I said, putting my cigarette out.

"Cool. Apartment 224. I'm gonna go watch my roommate unpack," Clive said with a relaxed, cross-grained laugh.

I laughed as well.

"Well, welcome to Yucca," I said.

"Oh, I've been here before," he said as he walked inside.

My roommates, not always eager to meet new people, declined the invite. I accepted and woke up the next morning naked on Clive's couch next to some blonde with big tits and rug burn. I remember falling down the stairs, and I remember snorting OxyContin off Ronald Reagan's Hollywood star. It was the beginning of something for Clive and me, our allegiance, and the destructive hell within me advanced like a fungus. The Zimmermans had both, at some point, voiced their unfavorable opinion regarding all the time I started spending with Clive and the devil-may-care tilt in my personality. It's not that they didn't like him. They mostly got along fine with my new ally. Hell, they even went along for the ride on occasion, mostly Peter. Equitably, though, in their eyes, Clive wasn't a positive influence on me, and he had the tendency to rub people the wrong way from time to time, even them. Clive was intense, abrasive, vulgar, and . . . dangerous. He was a harvest to handle, but I didn't care about that. He was willing to initiate certain behaviors that I had previously been afraid to. It made it easier for me to dare. I admired his indifference to outside judgment, and his definition of loyalty—that was the kicker. He was unceasingly honest, always had my back, and never judged, while at times, I felt the towering stare of the Zimmermans' arbitration. They meant well. I'd been looking for unbreakable camaraderie since I was eight years old, ultimately basing all my decisions regarding friendship on one question: If the lion came back, would they leave me on the floor, or would they bash his fucking head in? I knew what Clive would do. Peter and Ray, I wasn't so sure anymore. I still loved those guys, still wanted them in my life. It's just that I wasn't going to let them stop me from taking the campaign to the next level, whether it was by myself or with Clive. My more frequent drug use and alcohol consumption weren't helping things—a bigger problem disguised as a solution. I was still looking for answers to my past, an understanding of why the lion could do what he did and not pay the price . . . I mean, *really* pay the price. While I already had a history of experimenting with drugs, I hadn't even considered certain narcotics until I met Clive. Crack cocaine, ecstasy, OxyContin; I even smoked heroin, for God's sake. We'd go on two-day benders and completely forget about everything. He helped push me to that edge, weakening the absurdness of my surface admirable resolve. At the beginning I held strong, passing on many of his offers to scream in the devil's face. But little by little I gave in to the invitations, and my desires.

We are who we are.

On his own, Clive moves in the same venomous slither, willing and able to spit his native penchant for bane right between the eyes of the world. But for me, I need to be able to look over at my accomplice, to see on *his* face the same devilish curiosity that I've embraced at that defining moment of good or evil, reassuring me that *my* deeds, right or wrong, are not just *my* desires. And perhaps I was someone that Clive needed, a protégé of budding tyrannical desires to be encouraged through the blackness and the reward that lies within the tests of impulse. We ran everything up the flagpole—booze, drugs, violence, sex. When there was no pole, we constructed one. When there was no flag, we'd bind one. I'm a wolf in sheep's clothing. Clive is the wolf who wears a T-shirt that says, *"I'm the fucking wolf."* I'd never find a more dangerous and loyal friend, one I vowed to never let go of, no matter what. Three months after I met Clive, his roommate, Samuel, moved out, and I moved in. That's when Yucca *really* became ground zero.

6550 YUCCA STREET

YUCCA STREET IS off Whitley and Hollywood Boulevard in the notorious Yucca Corridor. It has a reputation of being a neighborhood seduced by drugs and gang violence. There are statistics to prove it. When Bartolo didn't answer his phone, Clive would sometimes walk down to the corner to buy drugs for us. He was better at handling situations like that.

The apartment building had evenly harmonized itself with the apocalyptic theatrics of the neighborhood around it—our own private version of bent city life. It wasn't like I'd ever experienced five-star living quarters before, but with Yucca, I'd never lived in such a comically humble abode. The desperate blue carpets that struggled to run the length of the halls were paper thin and pulled, stale and spotted, stained with shame and atrocity by the dilettante pathfinders of life's storm before us. It reminded me of the carpet in my brother's room on Granite Street. I'd walk the narrow, café-au-lait-painted halls, intrigued by the brand of humanity observed in passing, mostly degenerates like me, poster children for the lost and the leery. They were the bottom 1 percent, ne'er-do-wells only interested in satisfying a fiendish decadence. At least the bar was low. The outside of the building was equally uninviting, finished with a dense stucco covered in yellow acrylic. It was a phlegmy yellow—a thick, viscous substance dangling in the respiratory passage in the back of the city's throat. Most evenings there was a bevy of rackety tenants shaking the mezzanines, competing to see who could be the most turbulent in the witching hour. Clive and I, on many occasions, established that we could just as easily find or create trouble while cutting loose at our humble abode as we could painting the town a merry fucking red.

Up one floor to the left was Gus's apartment, or it used to be. Gus was sloppy, an overweight aspiring filmmaker from New Jersey. He'd evacuated the Eastern Seaboard for a run at God knows what on the West in a town that feeds on the anemic—arrived about two years ago with a high school friend of his, James. Then the drugs took him and raped him. That slipshod, chubby teddy bear transformed almost overnight, a mutation of the dire kind. He stopped chasing his dream, started chasing the high. At some point, *everybody* stops caring; it's a familiar story, one of life's repeated plagiarisms.

James's tenure was short-lived, about three months. He refused to witness the daily decomposition of his dear friend, Gus. By the time he flew the coop, Gus could barely communicate, whacked out on OxyContin from dusk till dawn. A week after James left, I clocked some funky white bird with dreads on their balcony—a real dirty son of a bitch. He was way out of place, even for Yucca, nervously scanning the courtyard to see if anyone had noticed his sudden arrival. Gus walked out behind him, looked like he hadn't showered in weeks. His bloated eyes were that of the dead and his shirt was torn. His jaunt was sluggish, the left side of his face swelled and bruised. Dreads snapped on him.

"*Get the fuck back inside, bitch!*" he yelled.

So much for being inconspicuous.

Gus shakily complied while Dreads pushed him back into the apartment, still yelling as he closed the slider, silencing the violence. I noticed a nine-millimeter Glock in the back of Dreads's pants. Turns out Gus was in the hole for a couple grand, so the ruthless drug dealer and his crew commandeered the apartment, used it to distribute drugs to the slavish trust of Los Angeles. They kept feeding Gus pills to keep him comatose and quiet, a prisoner in his own home. He couldn't do a thing about it. He was fucked up and dried up and, in the end, turned up with pennies on his eyes. He'd been dead a week before his kidnappers even noticed. By that time the cops had suffocated their enterprise.

I wondered about Gus's family—if he had any—about how they must have felt losing their son, brother, cousin, nephew in such a graphically sad and demoralizing way. I can't imagine being the parent of a child who would succumb to such a fate, unable to protect them.

The apartment underneath us was occupied by Rowan, Kyle, and Beetle, all botched attempts at human reproduction. Rowan was heavyset, six foot four with shaggy blond hair down to his chin, looked like an overweight Kurt Cobain (we called him Fat Cobain). In conversation he looked right through you, as if you were made of glass, speaking directly to whatever fell behind you.

Kyle was the wannabe lunatic, artist-type guy, his actions premeditated. He wanted people to think he was weird, a deep artist that no one could understand. But he was talentless. Hollywood was full of guys like that. He had greasy black hair and always wore a bow tie, looked like a more bedraggled Pee-wee Herman. He decided to draw on the walls in our apartment one night with a black Sharpie. Clive was being Clive and egged him on. I came home from work to find a path of thick black scribbles on the walls in the living room. It looked like

Jackson Pollock had performed an abstract expression on them, but the dead version of him, with no arms—a dead Jackson Pollock with no arms. Kyle explained that it was the map of a place called Gargantuan, a made-up world that he'd invented in his stupid little brain.

"It's the future," he said, whatever that meant.

The other roommate, Beetle, we hardly ever saw. A disturbingly quiet Native American who shaved his head with a butcher knife, always had spotted wads of toilet paper to cover up the nicks. He never made eye contact and always carried one of those toy pinwheels around with him, a red one. You'd have thought Fat Cobain was his racist guardian the way he spoke to him.

"Get the fuck back in your room, Tonto," he'd say.

Beetle would comply without complaint or defense, like a pet. He'd close his door and turn on the carnival music. It was rare that Clive and I would end up in their dungeon—only on the really dark nights when we ran out of money for drugs. It was a passive welcome, always met with a twitch, an odd smile, and the devilish chants that whispered from some hidden boom box we could never find. Their apartment was filthy, lunatic, the interior theme of an unlicensed mad scientist's lab. The kitchen counter was covered with experimental jars full of strange, cloudy liquids and small stuffed animals—lions and tigers and bears, oh, shit. The lights were never on, never worked, candles carelessly scattered about on paper stacks waiting to be tipped. Such a fire would leave the world a safer place. The dishes were piled high in the kitchen sink, covered with year-old grease and grime that had clearly murdered the china. It was odd that they had any kitchenware at all. There were stacks of it, like they'd won a fine dining set on some game show where you spin a wheel. I tried to use the bathroom once,

got the door open about an inch before the scent of formalde-
hyde, roadkill, and year-old shit singed the hair in my nostrils.

"Dude, what the fuck is up with your bathroom?" I asked
with watered eyes.

"Yeah, don't go in there," said Fat Cobain.

"No problem. Smells like dead teen spirit," I said.

He didn't get the joke.

And forget about finding a clean place to sit. The furniture
was covered in newspapers and magazines, fastened to whatever sticky substance lay underneath it. Occasionally you'd sit
on a moist spot. Clive and I had pretty thick skin but these
spawn-of-shit monsters were not part of the cast we wanted to
borrow sugar from—I'd have never gone down there without
Clive. After Fat Cobain decided to show us the bloodstains on
his samurai sword, we decided it would be best to avoid that
particular corridor of the pasty, yellow trough we called home.
About a month later they all disappeared.

Who the fuck knows and who the fuck cares?

Gina, Rene, and occasionally Lisa lived in the apartment
directly above us, another batch of East Coast hunters of the
great western dream—New Yorkers. Rene was sweet—short
and pudgy, big stoner, no ambition. Gina was veritably Italian,
thick Jersey accent, curly black hair. We developed into a mod-
erately chummy cartel, frequented neighborhood dives together
and whatnot. Then Clive pissed them off and it all fell flat and
fizzled. Gina and Rene called me, something about Clive stealing their weed, said they confronted him and he started pointing in Gina's face, told them both to fuck off. *Aggressive* was the
word they used. I was having sex with my girlfriend at the time,
Kelly. I cut them off, told Gina and Rene to take a piss.

"Not my problem," I said. "I'm in the middle of having sex,
for chrissake."

Their other roommate, Lisa, wasn't around all that much. An adrift, sexy little rose with miles and miles in her eyes. She looked like she'd hitched a ride on the Mötley Crüe tour bus and remained there for back-to-back U.S. tours. The quintessential rocker chick—thin, tan, tatted, pierced—whose idea of a career was hanging out with celebrities. I can only imagine the things she was willing to do to gain admittance into their world.

When Lisa wasn't partying, she was depressed and delicate, eyes full of sadness and a lack of sleep, a lost little girl with a frail frame that struggled to carry the weight of betrayals from her past. I wondered what her relationship was like with her father, if she had one, her brothers, if she had any. She was always so eager to please men. I would intentionally ignore her because every other guy groveled and drooled. I didn't want to stand in line at the deli counter.

She noticed it, so in turn, she ignored me back. That was basically our relationship. I held her hair while she puked once. She was shirtless. I didn't even try to take advantage of her . . . thought about it.

She came by with some vodka one day; she did that sometimes, when no one else was around to give her attention. Mostly she would stand in the doorway and act as if she wanted to come in but never would. When I opened the door, her smile was crooked and needy, and she made eye contact in short bursts. I asked her to come in. We talked about music and how she had just broken up with some B-level actor, Jeremy something.

"Wanna watch a movie?" she asked.

"Here?" I asked.

"No. My place. Gina and Rene are back East."

"Yeah, sure."

I made us a couple vodka sodas. We drank them pretty quickly, put on the movie *Heat*, then laid on her bed. Her room was naked, no pictures, no accessories, just a mattress with a white comforter and sheets and a TV on top of a white dresser. There was an open suitcase, torn, alone on the floor at the other end of the room, clothes hanging out. She nestled her back up close to my front, her arms curled into her chest, holding on to what was left of her virtue. I wrapped my arms around her, clutching enough to let her know that I understood her need for physical collision, her need to please, her need to be seen. She smelled like the sun had fucked her skin. It made me hard. As I felt a tear drop to my arm, Lisa reached back and grabbed my cock. I turned her toward me, kissed her as she cried. It made me even harder. Then, I don't know why—trying to be noble maybe—I grabbed her hand, gently squeezed, and raised it back up to her chest. I couldn't tell if she was offended or relieved. She cried harder, buried her face in my chest. I stroked her hair, said nothing. Lisa needed someone to give a shit, not roll her over and dip it in for sport. She'd been on such a long bender honeycombed with loveless sex, endless drugs, and empty rock-and-roll promises. I was familiar with some of the pain she felt, the longing for someone, for something to remain, and I chose to admit it to myself at that very moment. I held her in my arms as she cried herself to sleep. I stayed for a while, wondering what her pain was about. I didn't know everything there was to know about Lisa. That was the thing with people you met in Hollywood; you never really knew the whole story. Why they were the way they were, or what they were running from. But you also didn't really want to know, for fear that it would make you look a little too closely at yourself, and you might not like the things you found. Some people can handle the truth about themselves, some cannot.

I half-covered Lisa with her pale-white comforter; the TV was still on, the only light in the room shining a lazy smile on her tired face. I paused in the doorway, noticed her shaved pussy under the tiny shorts that were loose on her inner thigh, and my hard-on was back.

Well, I tried.

I walked back over to the bed, dropped to my knees, and kissed her neck. She awoke, responded by pulling her shorts down. I got on top and put it in, because I'm a salaciously sexual zealot. Our faces were close. Our eyes were locked. It was sweaty, it was rapid, it was dirty—it was fucking, and I came inside of her. We are who we are.

I only saw Lisa one other time after that night; she looked more lost than ever. This was the unfortunate essence of the Yucca Corridor. If you've got too much time on your hands living in such a place, you start intentionally misplacing little pieces of your self-respect, your decency; it's pure choice. The demons, they sense this . . . and they can be fun to play with. Whatever you want them to do, they'll do. Demons say yes to everything. But sometimes those demons will find a fuck buddy, impregnating an amalgam of reasons why one should skirt the very edge of death. When those demons harvest and multiply, then you're outnumbered, then you're fucked. They'll follow you everywhere you go; you smell them on your clothes, in your hair, on your skin. You taste them in your mouth. Those demons will take everything you've got and come all over it.

9:50 PM – AUGUST 13

CLIVE CAME OUT on the balcony while I was reminiscing about the early days of Yucca—the happy harm of it all—and my old roommates.

"What up, boy?" he asked.

"Just chillin'," I responded.

"Where the fuck is that cab?"

"It'll be here soon. Don't disappear again."

Clive just smiled.

We both lit up a smoke. I pulled out my phone, texted something to Peter.

Hey, guys. Just reminiscing. Been a while. Hope you're both well. Playing at the Whisky tonight. Eleven-ish. Will put you on the list.

"Peter and Ray?" Clive asked.

"Yeah," I said.

The last time I hung out with Peter and Ray was at Barney's Beanery. Clive wasn't with us. Things would have gone differently had he been there . . .

I never had luck at Barney's. With girls, with getting the bartender to notice me in a crowd. I was out of shape at the time, sloppy. That could have been it. You're easy to avoid if you don't keep up on your looks in Hollywood. Either way, the place felt like a fraternity that everyone else in Hollywood belonged to but me. And the floors were sticky. With every step the soles of my feet tore up the cellar's skin, like a bad wax job, each peel evaporating the smell of rancid, stale beer.

The crowd hovered over the barstools like heavy branches. It was packed. It was loud. Only hot girls and tall guys were being served. I hate trying to get the bartender's attention, especially in front of people I know. Every time my hand-raise or call to the barkeep is ignored, I shrink, an unimportant loser not worth the drink-slinger's eyes, king of kings, queen of queens. Now, if I had a shotgun resting on my shoulder . . .

Get me a beer, motherfucker!

That'd move things along.

After ten minutes, the bartender—shorter than I—finally looked down at me.

"Whataya have?" he asked.

"I don't know . . . for you to take my order in a timely fashion," I said.

"You say an old-fashioned?"

If I punch him in the throat, the night is over . . . That wouldn't be so bad.

"No . . . I said . . ." I thought about repeating myself, then, a little louder, "Pitcher of Miller Lite and a shot of Patron, please."

He didn't even respond. I looked around. Not one person was looking at me. The bartender did the work, took my money, and moved on. It was our third pitcher in the last half hour. I can only handle crowds when my face is numb. I took the shot of Patron and walked back to our table.

"You smell like tequila," said Ray.

Fuck off, Ray.

Ray's roommate was with us, Contra Ben, not to be confused with Little Ben. He was black market all the way, always looking for an angle. I liked that about him, but Contra and I didn't hit it off well. He thought I was a drunk, trouble. One of the first times I met him, we argued about football, the Patriots and Raiders' famous tuck-rule game. It was an aggressive argument. He was the Raiders fan. I didn't give a shit about football, but I'd grown fond of confrontations. I was hammered, abrasive. He was defiant, a know-it-all, and didn't expect such heat. Ray told *me* to calm down, said *I* was being a dick.

Contra was a James Dean type, an actor, good-looking, hailed from one of the Carolinas, had a thick accent. He was devious, clever, intriguing without trying. He couldn't help himself. But he also had a plan, something about vengeance and corporate conspiracies. He'd lost someone close to him, an uncle. As the story goes, Contra's uncle was found dead shortly after discovering detrimental information about the brake pads that his automobile company used. The pads were faulty, and the company knew it, and they hid it from the public. Cars crashed, people died . . . *kids* died. Two weeks later, on his way to the local newspaper to let the cat out of the bag, he was found with his car wrapped around a tree. Contra was thirteen when it happened, and he was 100 percent convinced that it was foul play. He preached about one day finding out who was responsible, handling it accordingly. I believed every word of it. Most people thought Contra was a crazy conspiracy theorist, but I couldn't get past the determination within him. He wanted justice. I wanted it for him. But we didn't like each other.

I sat down. Peter, Ray, and Contra were playing pool, all wishing I wasn't there, knowing it was only a matter of time before I fucked the night up. I was aware of the distance and resented it. That's where it started, when the whole world was against me, in that sector of the night when I held their fear and annoyance in the back of my throat like the drip that slides into a taste of numbing cocaine.

"Am I the only one drinking?" I said.

It didn't land. Their lack of response was telling. I went to the bathroom to take another bump. As the night wore on, I spilled a few drinks, got ignored by a few struggling actresses, mad-dogged a few confused patrons. I was about to hop the cue over the nine and put the eight ball in the side pocket when some asshole in a baggy sweatshirt bumped me on the way to his table. He walked past like it never happened, like I wasn't there. Just like the bartender who didn't see me, like the girls who didn't see me, like my songs that no one wanted to hear.

"Trying to play a game here, asshole," I said, approaching the enemy's table.

"Oh, shit," said Peter.

"Jake," said Ray.

The away team stood up from their table, one small, one medium, one large. Peter, Ray, and Contra Ben intervened, slowed the pace, turned to me with a condescending voice.

"Calm the fuck down, Jake," said Ray while Contra shook his head. "Every fucking time we go out, you pull this shit. You're changing, man," said Peter.

They'd witnessed my banishment from a mass of tea and tavern. There was Lava Lounge, Boardner's, The Dresden, Rainbow Room, Burgundy Room. The list goes on and on, not always my fault. If you asked Peter and Ray, they'd say something else.

They dragged me outside, where I managed to piss off another group of Barney's long-standing members. When the scuffle broke out, Peter and Ray bailed, leaving me to fend for myself against a company of four. All I could do was cover up and throw an occasional haymaker. I was getting bounced around like a pinball until Contra saved my ass. He dragged me over to a cab while I let the world know that it'd hit me with a cheap shot. Now I *had* to like the guy. He couldn't leave me behind. I had to respect that. I smeared my bloody knuckles across the bright yellow of the cab as he wrestled me into the back seat.

"Where are those motherfuckers?" I kept screaming. "They fuckin' left me!"

Contra—a crack shot with the ladies—somehow managed to lure a beautiful blonde with him in the process. Just another pretty girl mortified by one of my tirades. I found myself appalled by my own admiration of his ability to walk and chew gum in the midst of such chaos. Contra did his best to calm me while pleading with the cab driver.

"Look here, man. I'm gonna need you to drive faster," he said. "Yucca Street. Please."

The cab stopped in front of my apartment. Contra opened the door and shoved me out. He couldn't wait to wash his hands of the Jake he'd gotten all over him. There I was, heated and alone in the Yucca Corridor. I thought about walking to the corner of Hollywood and Whitley to buy drugs, but that was Clive's role. My entire body felt like fishing line attached to a marlin on the run.

Clive wouldn't have left me there.

I called a cab, hitched a ride to Ray and Contra's place.

"Fourteen Molly Drive," I said.

I arrived with only a pause to pay the driver. I ran up two flights and started pounding on the door. They had to open it.

"Dude, what the fuck is wrong with you?" said Ray.

"You're out of control, Jake," said Peter.

I heard them, but the wound in my back still burned like it'd been rubbed with lemon pulp.

"*You fucking left me there!*"

Contra was nowhere in sight, probably in the back hanging up the brothers' turncoats. I pleaded for answers different from the logical ones they were giving me, lost in such defeating madness that I'd failed to notice they had shut the door.

"Get the fuck out. We're done with you," was the last thing I heard.

Death punch.

I punched the stucco wall on my way out, hard as I could, signing off with blood and flesh. Like an angry hunchback, my shoulders led me home. Somewhere between sadness and hatred I bounced psychotically back and forth, crying, growling, raising my voice up to the speckled sky. I stared down cars and passersby, begging for someone to look at me wrong before I finally calmed enough to realize that I'd ruined something painted and kept in museum.

I went to the corner of Whitley and Yucca, bought an eight ball, went to my apartment, and threw the door open. Clive was on the couch reading Homer's *Odyssey*.

"What happened?" he asked.

When I told him . . . it was the look in his eyes. I'd never be able to defend Peter and Ray to him again, no matter how much I tried to explain their actions. And although I did question their loyalty, I still couldn't let them go, reminding myself that *I* pushed them away with my manifold of transgressions. They grew tired of bailing me out of trouble, dealing with such self-destructive bullshit. Little Ben had landed another promotional job that took him on tour across the country, this time with Pepsi, so he wasn't around anymore—he never really bore witness to the details of our disbandment. In the past, when friends fell by the wayside, I'd brush it off, tell myself it was for the best. I wouldn't fight for it. I couldn't do that with Peter and Ray. I loved them too much. And they had a point; I was a handful.

My phone rang.

"Hello. Yut, be right down," I said to the voice on the other end.

I turned to Clive.

"Cab's here."

We blew down a few lines before continuing the night. Next stop, Tricia's house, a girl from Clive's past. We got in the cab. The Doors's "Riders on the Storm" was on the radio.

"Santa Monica and La Cienega," I said to the driver.

"Those guys still love you," said Clive, referring to Peter and Ray.

"Yeah, maybe." I turned to the cabbie. "What's your name?"

"Mahkbesh," he said.

"Nice to meet you, Mahkbesh. I'm Jake. This is Clive."

Mahkbesh looked at me awkwardly in the rearview mirror. He hesitated but responded.

"You have address?"

I turned to Clive.

"What's the address?"

Mahkbesh gave me another look, then looked at Clive and squinted like he'd seen him before, then back at me.

"It's in your jacket," said Clive.

I reached in my right jacket pocket, pulled out a piece of paper.

"Three seventy-five North La Cienega," I said to Mahkbesh.

"Okay," said Mahkbesh.

"You put this in my jacket?" I asked Clive.

"No. You did."

"Oh . . . Don't remember doing that."

"I know you don't."

I'd been forgetful lately. Lack of sleep was catching up to me.

"So, who's this chick, Tricia?"

"Chick I used to work with at Miyagi's."

"Ah, this ought to be interesting. You guys hook up?"

Mahkbesh thought I was talking to him. "What's that?"

"Sorry, not you, Mahkbesh."

"We hung out for a bit," Clive said.

"She got any cute friends?"

"She did."

Clive leaned his head against the cool of the glass, the passing flashes of artificial subculture lost on him as he drifted off to somewhere else, thinking about another time altogether.

Amid Clive's first stretch in the city of fast nights and days of rigor mortis, he'd worked as a server at Miyagi's on Sunset. Parallel to the levels of madness that he and I were accustomed to, Clive's days at Miyagi's were equally bats in the belfry. He ended up getting himself into trouble, broke some guy's jaw, some model. The guy filed a lawsuit against Clive for taking away his ability to earn a living, so he exited stage left for a while.

"Hey, what time is it?" I asked.

I looked at Clive's watch. Ten fifteen.

The cab stopped.

"Sixteen thirty-five," said Mahkbesh.

I handed him a twenty.

"All set," I said.

Mahkbesh tilted the rearview mirror as Clive and I got out of the cab. What big eyes he had, so white, so bright. I closed the door. Mahkbesh tore off to find his next commuters with a past.

"This it?" I asked.

Clive stopped as he stepped up on the curb. There was pain on his face, the kind only love can cause. Then, I remembered who Tricia was. Tricia was Pa-tricia.

"Mate," I said.

"Yut."

His eyes still locked on the pale stucco building in front of us, looking up at the third-floor window to the far right. There were no lights on. It was dark (in-between-tenants dark). I'd never met Patricia, only heard about her. She was before my time, during Clive's first visit to Hollywood.

"Is this Patricia's place?" I asked.

"Yut," he answered.

"It doesn't look like anyone is home."

I lit a smoke.

"Here," I said.

I sat down on the curb, lit another cigarette. Clive sat down next to me, left his cigarette burning on the ground; he never touched it. I pulled out a flask of whiskey from my right inside jacket pocket, took a sip, and set it on the curb next to Clive. A young Hollywood couple walked by, good-looking, of course. They were holding hands, smiling, practically skipping. They mentioned the Whisky, said the name of my band. I may have started up a conversation with them had Clive not needed me . . .

Clive met Patricia at Miyagi's about three and a half years ago. The gist of it is, he and this other guy, Shawn the bartender, entered into a pissing contest—winner-gets-the-girl type shit. Shawn had been dating Patricia for a few months before Clive was hired. He made an immediate impression—as he does—leading those around him into temptation. Patricia couldn't help but notice, and curiosity brings the cat to chaos. Clive had a knack for that, titillating, selling danger. Shawn was a frat boy. Clive had art inside of him, albeit a childlike, sinister portrait; at times it was brilliant. Patricia was from Utah, a Mormon family. She was ready to release her pent-up-ness on the world, which meant reaping attention from wherever she could get it. In that sense she used Clive. He was straightforward and crazy with her. She was a virgin to his kind. It scared her, and she liked that. Shawn had a more plausible, more visible future, and that was also enticing, more the norm. Clive only had plans for acting, which was a long shot, and partying, which was a daily shot. When Shawn found out about Clive, he got physical with Patricia. When Clive found out that Shawn put hands on her, all hell went sideways. He walked up to Shawn at the beginning of a shift, didn't say a word. He got him real good with a right hand. Then it escalated, ended up in the parking lot, stopped the entire restaurant. The whole staff watched as they bludgeoned each other with meat fists. Shawn was a big guy, played football somewhere with a U attached to it. He could take a punch, but Clive was the better fighter, and they both took their licks. In the end, though, as satisfying as it was for Clive to come out standing while Shawn lay in a pool of his own blood—and some of Clive's—it was all for naught as Patricia ended up not being the bad-boy type as much as she thought she'd be. Something within Clive scared her that night. She ended things the next day, moved back to Utah about a month later. The kicker was she'd spent her last few weeks hanging out with Shawn. He'll never admit it, but I know that hurt Clive.

"So what are we doing here?" I asked.

"We?" he said.

Clive sometimes says things that you have to think about. So I thought about it. Then I remembered something else and forgot about what he said.

The blond girl at Reggie's! I knew I recognized her . . . Patrica's roommate.

I'd met her before, here, at a party with Clive about six months ago, before Clive overdosed. It was an awkward exchange.

My phone vibrated. I opened it. Another voicemail from my mother. There were several, all calls unreturned. I heard Clive's voice in my ear.

"You should call her back."

"Yeah, maybe tomorrow," I said.

"Take a bump."

I pulled the cocaine out of my jacket, pulled out my keys, and took two bumps.

"I don't want to be here anymore," said Clive.

"Neither do I," I said.

I put the phone to my ear.

Hi, hon, it's your mom. Just wanted to see how you were doing. It's been a while. Things are good here. Your brother's doing well, got a new job. Anyway, give me a call when you get a chance . . . Love ya.

Hi, hon, it's Mom. It's your dad's birthday today. Just tryin' to catch you. Give me a call . . . Love ya.

Hey, ole boy, it's Stan. Call your mother, would ya? She's worried about ya. All right, hope all is well, pal.

Hi, hon, it's your mom again. Hope everything is okay. I haven't heard from you in a while. It's your brother's birthday tomorrow. Might want to give him a call. Also, I got a call from your uncle Frank. He was asking about you. It's been a while since you've talked to anyone on your dad's side of the family. Thought maybe you'd want to give him a call. All right, sweetie, Love ya. Talk to you soon.

I avoided conversations with her because mothers *know.* She'd sense my ineptitude. She'd hear in my voice that pieces of me had fallen away. When we did talk, I'd give short answers, shading the furnishings of my bewilderment.

"Everything's great, Ma," I'd say.

Life's a peach.

She'd bring up my father. I haven't spoken to him since I was thirteen.

WILL WALDEN

THOSE VIVID MEMORIES, previously encoded and stored in the brain, they can revisit us from time to time. They invite themselves back into our thoughts whether we want them to or not, replaying a pattern of neural activity that selfishly reminds us to feel—once again—what it felt like in that clocklike moment, not caring whether that memory was exceptional or abominable, whether it was real or a dream.

I have this recurring nightmare where I wake up, still in my dream. My brother is crying, banging his fists on the other side of my bedroom door. He's calling for my father. But the sound is coming from inside of my head, the volume looping from low and deep to high and crackling. My eyes are open but I can't move. The calls for my father get louder, more distorted, warping my skull. Then Andrew calls *my* name. The door shakes. It's about to explode. He needs my help, he's begging, but all I can do is listen. All I can do is endure the feeling of a monster inside of me.

My father, Will Walden, was an affectionate man. He was average height, had shaggy brown hair and blue eyes, adorned with a full beard most of the time, sometimes just a mustache. Occasionally he would shave everything off and I wouldn't recognize him. Handsome, not stunning, he held the confidence of a silverback in a room full of house pets. It made him unafraid to be funny, but never at the expense of others . . . except my uncle Frank, who never got by without a ribbing. It was the greatest power in the world, how Dad could make people laugh, as natural as rain. He was smart, kind, and knew how to change a person's mind.

"It's important that you listen to what people have to say," he'd tell me.

"Why, Dad?"

"Because people want to be heard, Jakey boy."

Then he'd lean in, put his hand on my shoulder.

"You've got two ears and one mouth. So listen twice as much as you speak."

Will loved music and motorcycles, the cool stuff. Cool has its faults. Will was a drinker, a smoker, and had a wandering eye. But he was a great dad, and all I ever felt was love from the man. Mom and Dad separated when I was only one. But every Friday, Dad was there to pick us up, smiling the way I imagined Santa would smile. He was a gentleman, comical and sensitive . . . just a bit rough around the edges. Despite their disagreeable past, my mother and father still got along quite well. For us, I presume. I wouldn't say she was forgiving, but they remained friends. I respected that. Will had been unfaithful to Mom on more than one of his irrelevant business trips. Business-irrelevant trips, I should say. He was an engineer at a major American company in the computer industry, worked out of town, made a good living. Andrew and I weren't spoiled, but we had plenty. Dad bought me my first guitar when I was eight, a Yamaha, smooth black with a metallic white trim. I didn't really need anything else after that.

Anyway, Dad was a master at constructing would-be reasons for the higher-ups at his company to endorse his extensive travel log. Mostly, it was Puerto Rico, must have visited over a hundred times. But his motivation for travel was much more about romantic encounters than circuit boards and software. He had an honest and innate love for women and couldn't help but find something to appreciate in every one of them. Such a malignant yet contradictory respect, odd and gently poetic. Mom couldn't see past the marital indiscretions. The last straw came when he brought microscopic bugs home . . . in his pants . . . sort of a souvenir, I guess. Mom didn't see it that way. She filed for divorce.

Somewhere in between marital affairs and systematization meetings, Dad found the time to pick us up a few mementos, T-shirts emblazoned with the infamous coqui frog, a species of small frog native to Puerto Rico, onomatopoeically named for the loud mating call that the males make at night. Such souvenirs confirmed that we were never far from his thoughts, even in the path of his erotic conquests. I must have had a hundred of those T-shirts . . . one for every girl, I suppose. Wish I'd kept one.

Like any troubled man, there was a woman standing by who thought they could fix him, make him change his ways. My mother, his wife before her, his wife after. They all tried. But mostly, people can't change people. We are who we are.

Dad remarried when I was nine. Esther was her name. She was a bit odd . . . nice, but odd. She liked things to be quiet, wouldn't let me play guitar in the house, so I read a lot while I was there. An uptight germaphobe with an obsession for life-like dolls—the porcelain ones with the scary eyes that flickered when you walked past them, drowsy with the vibration of each step. She loved those dolls. I hated them. They scared the shit out of me; I thought they were going to kill me in my sleep. They asserted a dominance over the guest room, where I only wanted to dream, looking daggers right into my soul.

It guaranteed that I would continuously fall just short of the official act of sleeping—hell's own dolls. After a few visits consisting of little to no shut-eye, I decided to turn them toward the wall, but every time I went back, there they were, waiting with blank white faces, welcoming me with open eyes. Thank God their marriage didn't last. My father was different then. He was dull, not the aftertaste of himself when he was with her.

Despite all the changes that divorce can bring to a family—new wives, new husbands, new towns, new friends—despite the weight and strain that rests on the shoulders of patience and understanding, my father and I still remained close. I was still happy that he was my father. Then, our relationship disappeared—I was thirteen. I was invited to my first real party—Regina Hayward, an eighth grader. She only asked two seventh graders to come—Greg Dogard and me. Greg's parents and her parents knew each other. I was invited by default as his best friend. I didn't care how or why I was invited as long as Rene Teller was going to be there. I was in love with Rene Teller. When I asked my mother if I could go, she reminded me that my father was coming to pick me up that weekend.

"I *can't* miss this party, Ma," I said.

"Talk to your father," she said.

She didn't think it was fair to him. I was sure he'd understand. When I explained the situation, he listened attentively without interruption. I was afraid of the silence, that it wouldn't remain. I didn't want him to speak.

"I'm sorry, Jakey boy. I have a business trip coming up, and I'll be gone for two weeks, so if we skip this weekend, it'll be a month before we see each other," he said.

Death punch!

We went back and forth a bit. I pleaded but was sent back to the starting line every time—but this, but that. He had an answer for everything.

"But all my friends are going," I said.

"Jake, I understand, but it's not the last party that you'll be invited to. Your mom tells me you're pretty popular."

I should have told him about Rene Teller, about how I loved her. She was in my class, second row, third seat, brown hair, smelled like watermelon. It was her lip gloss. But I couldn't tell my father such things.

"C'mon, pal, I don't want to go a whole month without seeing you," he said.

"I wanna see you, too, Dad. It's not that. It's just—"

"The answer's no, Jake. I'm sorry."

I pictured Greg trying to make out with Rene at the party. I saw the way he looked at her in class. My torso stiffened. I felt the heat of an attacking poison running through my veins. Dad was trying to explain furthermore that it was my cousin's birthday, that I should attend. I snapped like a snake-headed grizzly bear, shattering his closing conjecture into fragments.

"Bullshit, Dad!"

The other side of the line went silent again, this time like the phone had been ripped from the wall.

"You're so selfish. All you care about is not looking like a bad father," I said, crying at the end of my words. "You cheated on Mom, remember?"

"Jake!"

"You don't think I know that you cheated on her and that it screwed up our family?"

"Jake, that's enough."

"That's why we're in this situation in the first place, because of you. And now you think it's okay to screw up my life again when I'm finally starting to make friends."

"Jake!"

I hung up, suddenly afraid. I knew I'd hurt him because he didn't call back. I told my mother that he'd agreed to let me go to the party.

"He did?" she asked.

"Yeah, he said to have a great time," I said.

I'm sure she called him, but she never mentioned anything more about the party. He mustn't have told her about our conversation. It was the last time I ever spoke to my father.

Shortly after that weekend, my mother set up counseling sessions with Dr. Withers, the school psychologist. He'd ask how I felt about not seeing my father anymore, made it sound like he was dead. It was all a bit dramatic, just trying to get in my head.

"I don't know," I'd say.

Dr. Withers didn't respond.

"Is that your father's jacket?" he asked.

I wore it to every session, wouldn't take it off.

"Yeah! He left it at my house the last time he was there," I said.

"And how does it make you feel to wear it?"

"Warm."

The sessions were pretty quiet. I couldn't wait for them to end. The counselor did most of the talking. I wouldn't really listen, mostly just pretend. I'd go through the motions, sigh. But I did cry once. I can't remember why.

10:46 PM – AUGUST 13

WE ARRIVED AT the Whisky, my heart racing from a quick bump.

"Hey, no drugs . . . please," said the driver.

"Yeah, sorry, mate," I said, and handed him a twenty. "Keep it."

We blasted out of the cab with moxie. I felt strong, confident, fully capable of delivering the goods to the stage. Over time, through experimentation, I'd figured out a concoction to help me perform—equal parts cocaine and bourbon. It's not that I didn't *love* being up there. I was just afraid to be. We stared incessantly at the patron saints of Los Angeles, calm on the outside, exploding on the inside. The wait-in-liners looked over because we were new faces in the vicinity; it was muscle memory. We perceived it to be much more than that, of course, as being high gave us the impression that we were important, legends in the ignis fatuus of our committed minds. Skipping the line, going right to the front, only added fuel to the fire. Boris the doorman held steadily, looked at me, didn't seem to notice Clive. Boris never said much, just wanted to see a pass. No pass . . . no pass. Boris is the prototypical burly Russian squarehead who only spoke with his eyes and head nods—six feet, two fifty, rotund in the middle.

"He's with me," I said, motioning toward Clive.

Boris looked at Clive, turned his eyebrows down, looked at me, looked at Clive, then back to me, then turned to let us pass. From the important side of the velvet rope, I turned around to witness the angry faces in line, that jaundiced look in their eyes, resentment and sometimes hatred at the thought of their unimportance. I enjoyed it all too perversely, getting off on the fact that some of them were there to see *me*. I needed those disciples, to dine on their affection, to suffer their love despite its ephemeral complexion.

The Whisky was packed and loud, an ugly sound. It was the band before mine, the Land Before Time. Their music was a mite heavier than their amps could handle. Clive was into it, but we tend to have an antithetical taste in music. While I enjoy the likes of Hendrix, The Beatles, and Warren Zevon, Clive is the august legatee of DMX, Slayer, and Kid Rock. He doesn't like my music all that much, but he's at every show. I looked at Clive's watch, 10:50 PM.

"You gonna get a watch?" he asked.

"I have a watch. It's on your wrist," I said. "What do we need a second one for?"

He didn't respond.

"I'm gonna head backstage and get ready. You wanna come back?" I asked.

"No, I see Max and Bill at the bar. Have a good show. Try not to fuck up."

I waved to Max and Bill. They were with two girls.

"Yeah, thanks, dick."

Max and Bill gave us a nod, looked at each other, whispered something to the girls. The girls looked our way. Clive went for the bar, his demeanor potentially caustic as usual.

From time to time I observe with a grin the way people notice him closing in. Even from a distance you can see them stiffen, preparing for a ball of fire rivaled only by the sun. It's on their faces, a naked and frightened expression in anticipation of his approach. Clive was intimidating to those he didn't love, and sometimes to those he did. That was an important and powerful part of the deception in his arsenal. He knew that, and he used it, to a titanic advantage. And so did I.

I went backstage. That feeling came over me—excitable boy. A high that titillated me even more than the narcotics that I had taken to get me there in the first place. I took a pull from my flask to calm the nerves, continued toward the dressing room, my eyes riding the blackened halls full of rock-and-roll history. Our dressing room door was open, Avi, Tim, and Hector framed inside, preparing for the show. Hector was twirling a drumstick in his left hand, tapping a two-four beat on the arm of the couch with his right. Avi, our lead guitarist, was running through some chord progressions while Tim—bass in hand—was staring at himself in the mirror, practicing his rock-and-roll faces, trying to keep the soft, dull beat of Hector's right hand. Tim had a penchant for flamboyant facial expressions on stage. Fans enjoyed it. We all gave him shit for it.

"And you wonder why everyone thinks you're gay," I said.

"Nice of you to join us, superstar," said Tim.

"Suck it, Snow White."

"Fairest of them all," said Avi. "Guitar's over there."

"We're on in ten," said Hector.

They're all good blokes, a bit of a pain in the ass at times, a bit square. Avi, he's like a brother. We have different lifestyles, but he's loyal. That's all I need in order to be loyal in return. But I can't ever show him who I really am, wouldn't want him to run the other way, think poorly of me. I'm afraid of losing people—to the truth, to death . . . especially death. I'd probably just pretend like it never happened so I wouldn't feel the pain. Most people can't do that. I wrote a song about it—"Nobody Dies in the End."

I picked up my guitar, thought about how far I'd come, from a small-town life to one dark Hollywood night.

GLOUCESTER, MASSACHUSETTS

WHEN I WAS eleven years old, my mother met Stan Wilson, a nine-to-five, blue-collar Joe barely in his forties. He was tall and good-looking, had a steady job, tanned skin, big hands, and a thick head of light-brown hair. He was quiet, a handyman at heart who loved getting lost in the work. My mother's youngest sister, Aunt Maggie, and her husband, Uncle Jack, introduced them. Stan and Uncle Jack worked together in Gloucester, both mechanical engineers. Mom was coming off an abbreviated marriage to the unconscionable bastard Jim Macker, stepfather number one, a real son of a bitch, aggressive. He got physical with Mom one night after she confronted him about cheating—I was nine at the time. I walked in the room and saw the look on my mother's face. It was fear that I saw, but also anger, like she was ready for a fight. It scared me—what else he might have done to her had she retaliated—so I crept up behind that motherfucker and smashed him in the back of the nuts with a whiffle ball bat. Son of a bitch folded like a lawn chair. Mom called the cops and Jim Macker hit the road. Good riddance. I found out later that I had permanently damaged one of his testicles . . . oops. He hit me once, told me books were a waste of time. Anyway, Mom deserved someone nice. I liked Stan. So did my dad. Andrew didn't care either way. He was fifteen at the time, getting into trouble, hanging out with a bad crowd. If he wasn't finger-banging girls at the movie theater or smoking weed in the woods, he was getting into fights, shoplifting, and running from the cops. One time he and a friend lit a bag of dog shit on fire, left it at the doorstep of some chick he was messing around with, just as a joke. She lived in an apartment on the second floor. The hall was carpeted. There was a fire. The cops knocked at our door an hour later, took Andrew away in handcuffs.

"We're investigating the incident as possible arson, Ms. Walden," said the cop.

That scared the shit out of my mother. My brother knew it was bullshit, told the cop to go kick rocks. My mother cuffed Andrew a good one in the back of the head.

"Show some respect, Andrew. This isn't funny. You're lucky you didn't kill anybody," she said.

"I think you better listen to your mother, young man," said the cop.

Anyway, nobody was hurt, the girl's parents dropped the charges, and the judge was about to give my brother a slap on the wrist. But at the hearing, my father stepped in and asked the judge to give Andrew community service. After that, Andrew went to live with my father and Esther in Townsend, Massachusetts (about thirty minutes away), for two months.

I wonder how he felt about those dolls?

It wasn't long before Stan was coming around regularly, every weekend. He'd drive two hours from Gloucester and two hours back to be with Mom for the weekend. I didn't mind. After six months, Stan asked my mother to marry him. That was fine, too. But then my mother told us we were moving.

Death punch!

She sat us down, gave us the hard sell.

"Now, you guys know I've always wanted to move back home. All my family's there," she said.

"What about Dad?" I asked.

"I've talked to your father and he understands. He thinks it's best, too. And he'll come get you every other weekend."

"What about Christmas?"

"He'll come for Christmas, too. He can spend it with us if he wants."

"This is bullshit, Ma!" said Andrew.

Mom told him to watch his mouth. He walked out of the room.

"Gloucester is a much better place to grow up. You'll see," she said to me.

"But what about my friends? What about Keo and Viet?"

Fitchburg was no prize, but it's all I knew. I didn't want to leave, didn't want to start over. Andrew obviously felt the same.

"I know it'll be hard, honey. But you'll see them when you visit with Dad. And they can come visit in the summer. And you'll make new friends in no time."

Right, because people are kind and caring and loving and generally fucking wonderful. Sure, this sounds like a breeze, Ma.

The thought of being the new kid made me nervous, and when I got nervous I had these tics—excessive blinking, constant flaring of the nostrils, sucking air through the corner of my mouth so much it made a slurping fart noise, scratching my arm till it bled. They were at an all-time high as I ran every horrible, embarrassing, and lonely scenario through the spin cycle of my cold-sweat, waterfall mind.

I rode my bike to Keo and Viet's house, broke the news, gave it to them straight.

"We're moving," I said.

They didn't take it well, remained quiet, the down and angry kind. It made me feel better, though. Such distress meant that they loved me. It's the only way you can ever really know such things, by the level of someone else's pain. It was hard to imagine everyday life without them. We were thick as thieves, a camaraderie that made me feel safe from the lions of the world, living less in fear, more in curiosity. I begged them—made them promise—to visit me in the summer.

"You can come visit whenever you want, stay as long as you want," I told them. "We can ride our bikes all over the place, go to the beach, maybe steal a few car stereos, maybe a car this time."

There wasn't anything I could say that would conjure our spirits from the grave. I cried in the rain as I pedaled home that day. A man pulled over, asked if I was okay. I rode faster.

Two weeks later, Mom and Stan were married at a courthouse, and we were off to a new town, crossing over the A. Piatt Andrew Bridge to Gloucester, bags packed, no turning back, our future up for grabs. It was midafternoon, the first Friday in September of 1987, the sky a stubborn middle-gray, refusing the sun. I slouched in the back seat wishing I'd been the one box that was left behind, forgotten, left to fend for myself. My head pressed against the cool glass, I watched the trees flicker past as heat filled the car with the smell of a warm engine. I thought about how much I missed Keo and Viet, how much I missed my best friends. Andrew was riding shotgun with his headphones on—Twisted Sister, Kiss, maybe. Mom was listening to a cassette tape of Barbra Streisand's "Everything Must Change," captaining our tiny red Nissan Pulsar in the far-right lane, perennially the pace car; speed was not her forte. As we got closer to Gloucester, the ocean conned me into good posture, its tranquility so pacifying. I rolled my window down to inhale the zephyr, a cordial welcome to help ease the anxiety of fitting into a brand-new life, of having to make a good impression on judgmental preteen decision-makers.

Yay!

Welcome to Cape Ann, the sign said. It all started to sink in, like heavy feet in wet sand—a new school, new people. I watched the boats. They looked frozen in place as we passed. The seas were calm, the wind was down. Then we passed Nichols Candies. We'd stopped there once before while visiting my mother's family. Some old man kept picking his nose in the store, fingering the fudge. I'd never seen someone so indecisive. Must've tainted forty pieces or so. I should've said something to that son of a bitch, but I was only seven at the time. Mom bought some fudge that day, peanut butter, my favorite. I didn't touch a one. My mother's entire family still lived on Cape Ann, some in Rockport, some in Gloucester. My grandparents were divorced but got along well. They were good, hardworking people who wanted to keep the family together regardless of their differences. How the hell they raised eight kids is a wonder.

I'd rather eat a raw pigeon.

In the past, we'd go to Rockport mostly, hang around Bear Skin Neck, walk through shops crowded with slow-moving tourists. My mother wanted to buy knickknacks as usual. She loved useless shit. It depressed me. I'd pull myself out of it by gorging on *untainted* fudge, rock candy, and saltwater taffy. We usually stayed with Grandma, sometimes Aunt Belle—she had a loft, and twin boys, Mark and Mitchell. Their dad wasn't around much—heroin addict—but was always kind when he appeared. They were good visits. But in the past I knew I would be going back home to Fitchburg come Sunday. This time it was different. This time I was already home, staring up at an entirely new moon, and I'd be waking up to a dimmer sunrise.

Gloucester is a small city, about thirty thousand people. It's a fishing town, an esteemed center of said industry, and a popular summer destination for tourists. Such scenic beauty also attracted and inspired the likes of many an artist whose work hangs in the galleries of Rocky Neck. We drove by the boulevard that overlooks the harbor. Flocks of townies walked along the esplanade at the edge of the sea as we passed the eight-foot-tall bronze statue of a fisherman dressed in oilskins, standing fastened at the wheel on the crooked deck of his ship. A plaque read: *They that go down to the sea in ships 1623—1923.* The phrase, clearly a memorial to those fishermen who had been lost at sea and a symbol of the hardworking people that made up the city.

We passed through downtown and into East Gloucester, a suburban section where Stan lived in a brown house—three levels, three units, our new home. When we arrived, the pit in my stomach pulled my intestines through my back.

I want to go home.

We parked the car in front, next to the cobblestone. Mom cut the engine. Streisand died, and silence prevailed as if life's saddest mime was sitting right next to me. Neither of us spoke or moved for an entire minute. Although Mom was excited about the onset of newfound love, it was bittersweet for her. She knew how hard this was on us. She was sensitive to it. Finally, Mom exhaled, then turned to us, her smile only half there.

"All right, boys. This i—" she began.

Before she could finish, my brother pulled his headphones down around his neck, opened the door, and got out of the car. I stayed, not yet ready to set foot on new ground, selfishly holding on to the possibility that this was all a dream. Mom stayed, too.

"You okay, hon?" she asked.

"Yeah," I said, head still pressed against the frigid pane.

She reached back, put her hand on my knee. I forced a smile, clutched the handle to the door, and looked at my mother. She only wanted to be happy, but so did I . . . but so did she.

"Let's go inside, Mom," I said with the same half smile, then opened the door.

Stan's sister, Mary, came down to greet us. She lived there with her husband, Joseph. They had the apartment directly across from ours on the second floor. I'd forgotten that my brother and I—on top of having to make new friends—would also be inheriting a whole new set of aunts, uncles, cousins, and grandparents.

Stan's ex-girlfriend lived on the first floor with her three daughters, Karen, Carol, and Laurie. Apparently someone forgot to tell Stan, "Don't shit where you eat." My mother didn't like that particular part of the arrangement, but Stan suffered the awkward encounters like a perfect gentleman, a smile and a modest nod in passing to avoid spousal combustion.

Our apartment was decent, clean, in a good neighborhood, and next to Swinson's Field—a park with tennis courts, a basketball court, a baseball field, and access to the woods, where teenagers would go to fuck. My room was upstairs next to Mom and Stan's. I had hoped for a little more distance, didn't want to hear them doing it. My brother's bedroom was on the backside of the apartment, down a stairwell on the first floor; it was secluded from the rest of us . . . as *he* was. Only a window separated him from teenage freedom, convenient for a sixteen-year-old boy with bubbling loins and a melting pot of new potential fuck buddies.

The big furniture had been moved in a week before. My room was almost fully set up—the bed, the dresser, even my fish tank was put together, clean as I've ever seen it. There was my guitar, a natural Fender acoustic/electric cutaway. That's all that really mattered to me, that and my books, lots of Jack London, Herman Melville, Rudyard Kipling, Mark Twain, H. G. Wells. The rest was still in boxes. Personal stuff, a statement of who I was, I guess. There wasn't much in there. Even the bed was made. Stan and my mother had gone the extra yard to make me feel comfortable. I lay down, could've slept for days, maybe longer, but couldn't close my eyes, so I picked up my guitar, practiced my scales. I noticed there were cubbies with small, stained shutters below the slanted wall on the other side of the room.

A place to hide.

I opened the wooden shutters, stuck my head inside. It smelled like pine. A can of paint and a few brushes sat to the far right. The rest was empty space, medium-lit, quiet. I grabbed a pillow from my bed, crawled in, laid my head down. My eyes gave in to the weight of the day, and the medium light was gone.

The yelling woke me; it was my mother and my brother downstairs. They didn't agree on much in those days. I crawled out of my hole. Mom's voice was louder now, Andrew's voice a bit lower than hers.

"We are all gonna sit down at the dinner table together tonight. It's our first night here, for Pete's sake," she said.

"Mom, I told you about this last weekend. Derrick's having a going-away party for me," said Andrew.

"Oh, my ass he is. You've already *gone*. Who has a going-away party for someone who's already gone? That's ridiculous! And that kid is nothing but trouble."

Stan stood by, not saying much. He was in a tough spot. He loved my mother but needed us to like him, too. Otherwise the next ten years would feel like . . . I don't know . . . more than ten. I tiptoed down the stairs to get a better listen.

"Mom, I already told him I would be there."

"And how is it that you expect to get there, Andrew?"

"I'll hitchhike . . ."

She laughed absurdly.

"My ass you will . . ."

Derrick Cridle was a world-class fuckup, a blonde eighteen-year-old with dirty fingernails. He hung with the younger crowd, those without older brothers or sisters. They had no idea how much of a loser he was. Derrick dropped out of school at fifteen, no job, no pressure from his fosters. They couldn't find a way through to him, so they gave up. Where does an unguided young man go from there? He'd been arrested a few times—breaking and entering as a juvenile, public drunkenness, some other minor infractions. Right before my brother turned fifteen, he and Derrick were pulled over for speeding in his foster parents' rusted blue Cutlass.

"Have you been drinking, son?" asked the cop.

"Evenin', copper! Not to worry. Only had a few," said Derrick.

The cop looked at my brother. My brother looked down at the floorboard. Derrick laughed.

"License and registration, please."

"Only if you show me a picture of your wife's titties first."

Andrew cringed. Derrick laughed harder. The officer punched Derrick in the face, then addressed my brother.

"What's your name, son?"

"Andrew."

"You live far from here, Andrew?"

"Not far, sir."

"Go on home then, son."

"Yes, sir."

My brother got out, walked the three miles home. The cop tore Derrick out of the car, put him in cuffs, and proceeded to beat the shit out of him.

"You're not going anywhere, and that's final," Mom said. "That kid is an absolute reject . . . and I told you that I didn't want you hanging out with him anymore."

I reached the bottom of the stairs, turned the corner.

"What's going on?" I asked, a curious cat when it came to the trials and tribulations of my brother.

I wanted to be like him.

"Nothing, sweetie," said Mom, then turned to my brother, pointed her finger at him. "You're not going, and that's final."

My brother left the room, walked right past me like I wasn't there. He was mad at my mom was all, not at me. I wish he'd looked at me, though. My brother was tough and strong and everybody liked him, especially girls. I wanted to hang out with him more, but I was only eleven. He was sixteen. While I was playing hide-and-go-seek, he was playing hide the salami. We hadn't gotten to know each other yet, not really. I only knew that he was angry and never wanted to be home, and very rarely wanted to be around me.

Stan, Mom, and I sat down for dinner. Andrew stayed in his room, a protest of social freedom. I'll bet he snuck out after everyone went to bed, climbed through his window and went . . . anywhere, just to smite my mother . . . and the rest of the world that cornered him.

IN WITH THE NEW

THAT FIRST WEEKEND in Gloucester I hardly left my cubby. Then Monday morning came. I awoke in a clammy sweat, my eyes were tired, and I had a boner that hurt like hell. My mother yelled from downstairs.

"Rise and shine, hon! Time for school."

My boner deflated. I opened the cubby, poked my head out. My bed was still perfectly made.

"I'll be right down!" I said.

I closed the cubby, lay back down on my sweaty pillow.

I knew nothing about my new school, where my class was, where my locker was. Nobody toured schools back then; you just went. I slept barely two hours, replaying worst-case scenarios in my mind. My nostrils flared, I frantically scratched, inadvertently held my breath a few times. I knew exactly what was going to happen on my first day in my shitty new school: Mom would drop me off at the curb, her demeanor a uniform of false nonchalance. She'd say good-bye but I'd be too busy preparing for my race across the blacktop to respond, trying to outmaneuver the blistering-hot, new-kid spotlight. I'd hope for the power of invisibility, then realize how stupid that was. I'd remain still, unable to take the first step, while Mom continued badgering me with good-byes.

"Honey, have a great first day. Hon? Jake?"

Then, the yard lady who organized the drop-offs would yell at me.

"Hey, shit stain. Yeah, you with the cowlicks. Get to class, and tell your mother to move it along. She's holding up the drop-off . . . And welcome to hell."

I'd aim across the school yard hoping my stride would fall silent on the torturous concrete stage. But like a big dumb fuck of an animal, every thunderous, block-footed step would sound off an attention-whoring honk, like those bike horns or those clown props. The distance from drop-off to the school entrance would feel like it was a hundred miles long. With every clunky footfall, their eyes would find me—the new guy with the hideous brown corduroys—because I looked out of place, nervous and sweating from the thought of their judging gaze. They'd be correct in their prudence, I'm sure. I'd go to the principal's office, ask where my classroom was, who my teacher was, tell the secretary that I'd be back, probably multiple times throughout the year. She'd find that odd. I'd go to my classroom, stop in the doorway, scared shitless to brave all the new faces. Students would pass me by, one by one, nudging the back of my shoulder en route to familiar chairs. In passing they'd be indifferent, and I'd hope for it to stay that way. I'd inhale, then exhale slowly, hoping it would last longer than it actually did, unable to snuff out the anxiety. Walking into class, I'd receive the same *who the fuck is this guy?* stare that I'd received on my amateurish stretch across the courtyard. The boys would want to kick my ass and the girls would wonder if I had a small penis, all laughing in sync at my cowlick-infested head. The teacher would introduce me, and no one would give a shit, or worse, everyone would give a shit. I'd then be inhumanely forced to stand—feeling stark-naked—in front of the classroom with my balls shriveled to a pea from the cold-knit brows that were squinting to find any sign that I was indeed a boy. I'd be asked to share things about myself, announcing where I was from and that my favorite color was black and that my favorite sport was avoiding situations like this and that I hated this stupid new town and this stupid new school and all of their stupid new faces and blah, blah, piss. Then I would sit down, bright red, still breathing, and the classroom would explode.

Thankfully, my first day didn't go the way my anxiety had imagined. I got through the front doors feeling quite invisible, in fact. My teacher's name was Mrs. Drake. She had white hair, loud shoes, and rarely smiled. She was afraid to show her teeth, revealing her true identity as the Big Bad Wolf. I was apprehensive about trusting her, but that had more to do with my last teacher. Ms. Morissey, fourth grade, the most beautiful teacher I'd ever seen, and a captivating speaker. My eyes stretched wide at the burst of her conviction whenever she addressed the class, words that came from someone else's pouty lips in that they were stern, factual, not soft and laissez-faire like her lips. I'd stare at her mouth, my gut hollow, never remembering exactly what she said. We'd talk one-on-one sometimes, life stuff . . . school stuff, too, but that was just for show.

"How is it possible that there is no Mr. Morissey?" I'd ask.

She'd blush, laugh, tell me we should stick to appropriate conversation. She was only saying that so the other kids wouldn't be jealous of our relationship.

"Sure, Ms. Morissey," I'd say.

I was first to class and last to leave, and an avid volunteer when it came to reading in front of the other students. You got to sit next to Ms. Morissey when you did that. I'd pretend to struggle with the words because she'd lean in close, place her hand on the small of my back while the tail of her cool, minty breath would drag across the side of my neck as she helped me sound out the words; I knew the words. Ms. Morrisey was tall, thin, and her shoulder-length blonde hair followed her down the halls like a loyal little pet. She wore silk blouses—a different color each day. My favorite was the white. It adhered to her body in such a way that made it difficult for me to stand up from my desk. I touched the silk once. After class I asked her to help me with a sentence. She leaned over. I reached out and caressed her shoulder. It startled her, and that was that. The next day Ms. Morissey met with my mother, recommended having a talk with me about proper student-teacher boundaries.

Death punch!

After all the times I'd been her daily helper, after all the laughs we'd had, the solitary moments we'd shared. Our relationship was only beginning to develop, and Ms. Morrisey ruined it.

Mrs. Drake was unimpressionable; she wasn't all that attractive, either. I took a seat, thank God in the back-left corner so the other kids wouldn't peg me with tight crumpled balls of paper that read, *Nice hair. Go the fuck back to where you came from, faggot.* The kid to my right was picking little seeds out of his hair, putting them in the pencil holder, that little concave inlet engraved in the desk. I thought maybe it was lice, so I slid my desk a little to the left. The sound of metal dragging across linoleum turned all eyes toward me.

Bricks in the wall.

"Sorry," I said.

Mrs. Drake continued, all eyes back on her. The kid with the seeds was still staring at me. He leaned in.

"They're seeds from the trees outside," he said quietly.

"Ummm . . . okay," I whispered back.

He stuck his hand out for a shake.

"I'm Greg, Greg Dogard." I hesitated, looked at the seeds. "I swear they're from the tree. It's not lice or anything, I promise."

"Yeah . . . Okay . . . I'm Jake."

"Where you from?"

"Fitchburg."

"Where's that?"

"Couple hours away."

"Cool. Why'd you move here?"

"My mom met this guy, he's from here. They just got married so we moved . . . Plus . . . I got into some trouble back home."

I don't know why I said that last part. It wasn't true, but I felt like I needed to add something.

"What kind of trouble?"

"Just some fighting stuff, no big deal, really. I'm not supposed to talk about it."

"Like you could tell me, but then you'd have to kill me?"

We both laughed. Mrs. Drake gave us a stern look as she kept reading.

"Anyway, my mom met this guy, Stan. He's my stepdad now," I whispered carefully.

"Cool. Where's he live?"

"Mount Pleasant Avenue."

"Madness . . . that's where I live, near Swinson's Field. I'm at ninety-nine. What number are you?"

"One fifteen, I think. Brown house."

"That's right across from the Munzes' house. They've got like eight kids or something."

"Whoa."

"You got a bike?"

"Yeah."

"We should ride down to Swinson's after school. Have you been there yet?"

"No, just got here Friday, haven't done much, really, unpacked and stuff."

"We should go there after school."

"Yeah, sure."

"Cool."

"Quiet!" said Mrs. Drake.

After class, Greg invited me to sit with him and two others at lunch—Eric Trayvo and . . . Nicole . . . Nicole Lewis. After meeting her, I wanted to spend weekends at school, study the subject of *her*, not eat, not sleep . . . till it killed me. She was a little taller than me, long brown hair, hazel eyes, dressed punky, and smelled like something sweet I'd never smelled before mixed with a little armpit sweat. Eric didn't say much, brooded, gave short responses. He was untrusting. I didn't like him. I asked Nicole right away what her favorite book was.

"*The Catcher in the Rye*," she said.

"One of mine as well," I said.

Nicole and I discussed other books, *Lord of the Flies*, *To Kill a Mockingbird*, ones that we'd revered. Greg and Eric could only watch; they had nothing to add. For all intents and purposes, they had disappeared.

I met Greg at the entrance of Swinson's Field after school. I got there first, waited on my silver and red Schwinn Predator with the hard racing seat. Greg showed up on a Huffy, green and white, soft seat, lame foam pad on the crossbar.

"Cool bike. You race or something?" he asked.

"Yeah, a little," I said. "But just for fun."

It wasn't true, just a better answer. I could handle a bike well enough, figured I could back it up.

"Cool. Let's go. I'll race ya," said Greg.

He took off without another word, down the long, graveled driveway, toward the entrance to the park. I roared after him, my tires spitting up rocks as I passed the white house on my left. At the entrance there was a large, oblong pole about chest level, grayish-blue, freshly painted. It went across the width of the driveway. You could either go under it or around it and through a four-foot-wide opening to the right. I gained some ground on Greg as he started to slow.

He's gonna go around.

Greg was pudgy, nonathletic. I jumped off my bike, tilted it sideways just before the pole. I would've been clotheslined had I not ducked. Greg almost tripped over his bike as impressed as he was. I pedaled like a maniac, full speed, refusing to look back. I passed the basketball and tennis courts on my right, continuing as the dirt road bent to the left. Just past the bend, a life of plush viridian took its last breath before the fall. There was high grass on the left and a rocky hill on my right overpopulated with tall trees. The dirt road bent to the right, then a long straightaway. I looked back—no Greg. I slowed, hoping he would catch up just enough to see how far in front I was. Five seconds, six, then he popped around the corner, still fifty yards away. I sped up. At the end of the straightaway, I came to the entrance of the baseball field, where I slammed on the brakes, skidding into a drift as the earth surrounded me in a puff of tan dust. The baseball field was straight ahead, well kept, ghostly empty, and as green as could be. I turned around to see if Greg was close. No sign of him.

"*I win!*" he said from over by the baseball diamond.

I pedaled closer toward the voice, around the corner. He was sitting on his bike at the end of the path, big smile.

"That's bullshit," I said.

Greg laughed his way toward me.

"That's my race, dink," I said. "No shortcuts."

I wasn't laughing. The air tightened. Greg and I weren't friends just yet.

"Aw, c'mon, man, I was just messin' with ya . . ." he said nervously, realizing that I had taken the race more seriously than him. "Nice move at the gate, by the way."

"Yeah . . . well . . . I figured I needed to make up some ground. You quick-started me."

"Yeah. You caught up, though. You're pretty fast, man."

"Thanks. Sorry I called you a dink."

That made us both laugh. It's awkward going from being angry to anything else without laughter. It eliminates the regret we feel in the silence. Greg took me back through the shortcut he used. The rest of the day he showed me around the woods, through the different paths where we could ride our bikes, explore. We stopped at a big net structure connected to four different trees—one in each corner making a perfect square.

"That's the Net," he said.

"What's it for?" I asked.

"Older kids *do it* there."

Sex in a net?

I didn't know much about sex, aside from weird feelings I'd get around pretty girls sometimes. My brother had some dirty magazines. The people in the pictures didn't look like they were being very nice to each other, grimacing in pain. I liked that part. It excited me.

"Hey, what's up with Nicole?" I asked.

"She's cool. A lot of the girls at school don't like her because she dates older guys," he said.

"How much older?"

"She's dating some kid from middle school right now, eighth grader. I don't think it's serious . . . I guess . . . I'm not sure, though. She dates a lot of guys, I think. Anyway, she thought you were cool."

"She did?" I could barely keep from exploding in my pants. "What'd she say?"

"Not much, just that you seemed cool. Why . . . You like her?"

"No!" I said quickly.

"It's cool, dude, everyone likes Nicole. But I wouldn't if I were you. Like I said . . . she's into older guys."

"Yeah . . . no . . . I mean . . . I think she's cool and all, but . . ."

"People think she's trashy, but . . . they don't understand her. She's got kind of a messed-up family life. I think her father's an alcoholic or something. I don't think he's very nice to her."

I wanted to kill her father.

"I better head back for dinner," said Greg.

"Yeah, me, too."

Back at home, my mother and Stan were sitting on the couch watching the news.

"Hey, sweetie," Mom said.

"Hey, ole boy," said Stan.

He always called me ole boy. I didn't mind.

"How was school today?" Mom asked.

"It was good," I said.

"What did you do after?"

"I was at Swinson's Field with a kid from school, Greg something."

"Was that the Dogards' son?" asked Stan.

"Yeah. You know him?" I asked.

"Not well. Seems like a nice family, though."

"He in your class, sweetie?" asked Mom.

"Yeah, he sits next to me."

"Oh, good," they both said.

"I'm glad you're making friends, hon."

"Yeah. What time's dinner?"

"Six thirty."

"Okay, be down in a bit."

I ran up to my room, thought about Nicole, crawled into my cubby hole, and imagined what she would look like the next day. She was different from any girl I'd ever met. And not just because she was older; she was thirteen, held back a year for poor grades. It was something in her eyes. They were deeper than most, filled to the lashes with more life than her age could boast.

The next day, Nicole wasn't in school. I sat quietly while Greg and Eric talked about baseball, football, other girls who were nothing like Nicole. I took inattentive bites of my roast beef sandwich as I watched the entrance to the cafeteria, waiting for Nicole to arrive.

She's probably skipping, hanging out with her older boyfriend who thinks he's some hotshot.

School was a mortuary without her. Eric asked me a lot of questions—where I was from, what sports I was into, had I ever been laid. I ignored the last one. He thought he was being funny.

"I heard you left Fitchburg because you got into trouble," said Eric.

I gave Greg a look. He looked down at his tray. I looked back toward the entrance to the cafeteria—no Nicole, just Mrs. Drake roaming, monitoring.

"My mom got married. Stan lives here, so we moved here," I said without looking at him.

"So you don't have a dad?"

Greg stopped chewing. I put my sandwich down.

"I have a dad."

"He a deadbeat or something?"

Greg should have said something, but he didn't.

"What does *your* dad do, Eric?"

While riding our bikes through the trails at Swinson's Field the day before, Greg had told me that Eric's father was out of work.

"What does that have to do with anything?"

"He out of a job or something?"

The conversation fell off. Greg finally opened his mouth for something other than to put food in, changed the subject, talked about female pop stars. Eric went on about how he'd met a girl in Canada who looked just like Debbie Gibson. That's when I looked back toward the cafeteria entrance.

"When's James coming back to school?" Greg asked Eric.

"Who's James?" I asked.

"My best friend," said Eric, sharply. "He got suspended for throwing a rock through the gym window. Fuckin' hilarious."

"You with him? Why didn't you get suspended?"

Eric looked down at his lunch tray.

"No . . . I wasn't there."

"Speaking of deadbeat dads," said Greg.

James was an only child, lived with his mother. His father was a homeless junkie who would occasionally show up at the house looking for cash to feed his habit.

"Shut the fuck up, Greg," said Eric.

"What? I'm just saying."

"Say it to his face."

Eric had a point. After the quiet, Greg suggested that we all go to Swinson's on our bikes after school.

"Ah, yeah, sure. Hey, have you guys seen Nicole today?" I asked.

Eric smiled at Greg.

"Leave it alone, Eric," said Greg.

"Not you, too," Eric said to me.

"Not me, what?" I asked.

"Nicole!"

"What about her?"

"You like her."

"I don't even know her."

"Yeah, but you like her."

"Do not."

"Eric, knock it off," said Greg.

Eric stood up, put his hands on the table, and leaned in. I could smell his breath—cantaloupe.

"You wanna pork her."

I bent the head of my fork and stood up fast, sending my chair back a few feet.

"*Fuck you!*"

Eric's expression was a statue of embarrassment and disbelief. He was stunned by the verbal backhand I laid across the features of his ego. The entire cafeteria stood tall, watching his face turn so red it was purple, his breathing so heavy that he couldn't speak. He just stared as if I shouldn't have dared—not the new kid.

I'll bury my fucking fork in your eye.

Greg was wide-eyed and pale, as if I had just revealed to him that, after trying my best to brush off her many flirtatious advances, I'd given in and fucked his mother. The cold, stabbing tap of Mrs. Drake's wrinkled finger on my rigid shoulder broke the tension and nearly broke the skin. She peered down at me through those Big-Bad-Wolf-disguised-as-Grandma reading glasses that hung on the tip of her nose while the stern exhales of her breath bent the cilia in her nostrils like tall blades of grass bathing in a hot wind. Her ice-blue glare burned through the lenses as she pointed to the door.

"Principal's office . . . now!" she said.

I waited outside of the principal's office, counting the times his secretary sighed and said, "Oh, dear!" I'd forgotten why I was there until Nicole walked in with a piece of paper in her hand. She gave it to the secretary.

"And you're late because?" asked the secretary.

"Doctor's appointment," said Nicole.

The secretary took the note from Nicole. I stood up.

"Hey," I said.

"Jake! What are you doing here?"

"Wasn't feeling well. I'm better now."

BLEACHER SEATS

TWO MONTHS IN a new town and a new school started to sink in. I considered Greg my friend. Discussions with Nicole had hit the penthouse-suite level, more personal, more flirtatious. My grades were okay. Things at home were good. My brother hadn't gotten into any trouble and Mom and Stan were happy. Nicole had broken up with her middle-school boyfriend, her third in two months and yet another douchey fuck-tard who couldn't beat me in a race if he had a motorcycle. The light was green. She smiled at me often, insinuating pearly bright thoughts of future hand-holding and tit massages over the shirt. We laughed a lot. That gave me confidence, even on days where my cowlicks—those godforsaken arching wooly branches that protruded from my scalp—were at their worst. My plan was to ask her to meet me at Swinson's after school. Then, I'd hit her with it. She'd never expect it, or hopefully, she would. We'd fall easily into one of our conversations about how her family didn't understand her. I would tell her that she's not like the other girls. She'd tell me how much she wants to be a writer, travel the world. I'd tell her, "If only the world could be so lucky." Hopefully, there would be no one else around to puke at the sound of such clichés. I'd go on about my past, a papier mâché history of who I claimed to be, spin a yarn about being a philanthropist, some bullshit about how I'd ride my bike through the scabrous back alleys of Fitchburg at night to do good after my parents fell asleep.

"I'd climb out of my bedroom window at night," I'd say.

"For what?" she'd ask.

"To feed the homeless."

"Weren't you scared?"

"Sure, but it was worth it."

She'd be impressed. I'd shrug like it was no big deal.

"I'd fill up my backpack with stuff from my house. Bread, cereal, milk, trail mix, fruit . . . you know, essentials that they didn't have to cook," I'd say.

"And no one tried to mug you?" she'd ask.

"I ran into a few tough situations, but I had a buck knife. I'd take it out and that was that. Plus, after a while, people started to recognize me. They realized I was just trying to help."

But that wouldn't be a high enough pedestal to put myself on. So, I'd thicken the plot. I'd tell her that one night I came across an entire family living in the streets behind the dumpster on President Street—a husband and wife and their three kids. The kids would be four, six, and ten years old—Markie, Danny, and Mable. The father, Benson, would have lost his job at the paper mill, and his wife, Patty, would have been diagnosed with multiple sclerosis—I didn't even know what multiple sclerosis was. I'd tell this to Nicole with a Shakespearean tear in my eye.

"I don't know, I just felt that I was meant to help them . . . So I started visiting them regularly."

Her eyes would water. Once again, I'd give a shrug.

"Where did you get the money?" she'd ask.

"Money from paper routes. Profits I made from selling the penny candy that I'd stolen form Bertha's Penny Candy Shoppe. It must have been three hundred bucks."

I did, in fact, steal from Bertha, but that was only because she was a thieving wretch. She was charging two, sometimes three cents for some of the "penny" candy that she had advertised. When I confronted her about it, she turned her nose up and shouted, "*Inflation*, you little *shit*," while waving her crooked middle finger in the air. Mean as a snake, she was.

"You're sweet, Jake, and brave," Nicole would say.

After wooing her with my manufactured noble past, I would ask her to be mine, and she wouldn't be able to resist leaning in for a kiss. Best-case scenario.

After school I went home, showered, combed my hair. I used my brother's gel, bathing each strand, adding enough weight to mat my cowlicks down. It took almost half the bottle, then some of my mother's Aqua Net hairspray, enough to sprout a small, pin-like hole in the ozone layer. With a finely crafted concrete helmet, I hopped on my bike and hit the road, leaving before anyone came home and started asking questions. I was nervous enough as it was.

Nicole was already there when I arrived, waiting for me on the four rows of silver bleachers by the baseball diamond. My eyes traced up from her lower back to her hair; she was wearing a purple flower behind her left ear. I approached quietly through the shortcut that Greg had showed me. Nicole rapidly tapped her right foot on the metal, creating a hollow, tinny echo that rang across the field. I stopped for a moment to notice her some more, just a little longer.

What if I didn't say a word? What if I just walked up to her, let my eyes say what I could never possibly say with words, then kissed her?

Then I came to my senses and realized that this earnest flash of time needed a downgrade in acceleration. Our romance was still in its infancy, after all. Better to not leap foolishly, lips first, into such a determining hour just yet.

What if she rejected my kiss? That would be the worst.

I had never even kissed a girl before. Only briefly had I fondled my first-grade sweetheart, but we had no idea what we were doing—I did love her, though. Jennifer was her name, but a French kiss was much more intimate than curious petting, mostly over the clothes. Try telling that to my first-grade sweetheart's parents.

Jennifer—my first love—and I used to shield ourselves at nap time in kindergarten, covering up with pillows during quiet hour, head to toe, until Ms. Raven bent the throttle overhead and caught us with our pants down. Three days in a row she'd witnessed the pillows wiggling and giggling as Jennifer and I tried to slither our way out of her skirt and my Wranglers without blowing our cover. It came to a devastating end when our love barricade came tumbling down. It resulted in a phone call to both sets of parents, which quickly steamrolled into an angry mom and dad on her end, an angry mom on my end, and an imminent and well-earned birds-and-bees-esque conversation between my father and me—excruciating but worth it. Jennifer was the first girl I'd ever loved. But this, Nicole, she would be my first kiss.

What will I do after that? Hump her?

I ditched the utopian-Hollywood course of action, continued on, walked my bike toward my bit beneath the trees. As her purple tulip brightened and grew in size, I started to sweat more. I lifted my right arm—deodorant check, all clear. Then the nervous tics—a swallow, a twitch, blink, blink.

Just breathe!

She was leaning forward, her chin resting in her left hand as she played with her hair. It reminded me of my mother. I used to twirl her hair when I was younger, maybe four or five. Nicole was wearing black jeans and a sweater that blended with the trees. I fought the urge to puke from nerves, then called to her.

"Hey," I said.

She turned to her left, her hand still on her chin, allowing only a sliver of her pearly white smile to shine through her ring and pinky fingers. She was happy to see me. While getting ready at home after school, I'd planned everything out, step-by-step. What I would say, how I would walk, even the way I would look at her. But when I got to the bleachers and tried to set my bike down, my pants got caught on the pedal. I wasn't paying attention to my feet because I was too busy keeping eye contact with her—it was in my plans to keep my eyes on her eyes the entire time. In retrospect that part of the plan was probably leaning more toward the creepy side than the romantic side—nobody wants to be stared at without intermission. As I tried to walk toward her, I fell to the ground in a dramatic and twisting reach for the stands, like an elderly person losing a handle on their walker and flailing desperately to find the shirt sleeve of their nurse on the way down. The silence was deafening. Then, Nicole began to laugh, and all of the fear and embarrassment went away as I remained comfortable on the hardened, cold winter floor. I joined in. We laughed hard together. It wasn't how I'd pictured it, but it was just fine. She stepped down from the bleachers, wiped a happy stream from her face, and gave me her hand. She was so damn beautiful. I was excited like I'd never been before. The laughter faded as I made it to my feet. Our faces were close.

"Will you go out with me?" I asked.

She looked at me without a word for seven seconds, then, she leaned in and kissed *me*—tasted like a grape Tootsie Pop.

The whole ride home my dick was hard and my stomach boiled. I ran upstairs and through the living room.

"How was your day, sweetie?" Mom asked.

"Great!" I said as I continued to my room.

I locked the door behind me, my breath heavy. I had to do something about the feeling in my gut and balls. I went into my cubby, pulled down my pants. It was a confusing but satisfying end to the day as my entire body convulsed in a way that kind of burned. I was expecting something to come out like in those magazines my brother had, but it didn't. I opened the cubby, lay on my bed, stared at the fish tank on my dresser by the door, and watched the three orange-and-white fish swim through the murky, unusually low-level water. They swam anxiously, like their world was closing in on them. I didn't think to do anything about it. I was still smiling, and my eyes felt heavy, then, the fish were gone.

WHAT KISS?

MONDAY MORNING I didn't see Nicole until lunch. Usually we hung out for a few minutes in the morning before class. I'd written her a poem and couldn't wait to show her.

Must be late today.

I was sitting with Greg and Eric at our usual table in the cafeteria at lunchtime when Nicole walked in, didn't sit, said hi, grabbed a juice from the cooler, and walked out. Eric didn't seem to give a shit. Greg looked sadly down at his food. I didn't say anything, played it cool, hadn't yet told the guys about our kiss; no way they'd believe me.

I went to Nicole's locker after lunch.

"Hey," I said.

"What's up, dude?" she said.

Dude?

"Umm, not much, just chillin'."

"Cool."

She never even looked at me, just gathered a few books and stared inside her locker. I wanted to bring up our kiss, maybe hold her hand, but I didn't want to be the pathetic weirdo who looked like he hadn't been in the big game before. Nicole was into older guys with much bigger bags of osculating experience, more mature, more in the know. I had to pretend that I had all of those things—the swagger of an all-knowing middle schooler with a pocket full of sensual escapades.

"Wanna meet at Swin—"

The bell rang.

"Gotta go," she said.

I felt like her little brother as I watched her walk away. I wanted her to turn around and look at me again, the way someone does when they love the other person. She didn't turn, and I went to class. What at once seemed mad-in-love poetic turned boldly apathetic.

How can someone's mind change so quickly? Surely I didn't dream this whole thing up.

Tuesday was much of the same. Wednesday she wasn't at school and didn't answer her phone. Thursday I couldn't run into her at school if she'd been the actual fucking school. It was a slow death. Friday morning I went to her locker but she wasn't there.

What the fuck?

I went over to Greg's locker. He'd been quiet all week, gave me a sullen look, took out a history book.

"Hey, have you seen Nicole?" I asked.

"No," he said.

"She's been acting weird lately."

"That's just Nicole. She gets like that when she changes boyfriends."

"Wait, how did you know about us?"

"Huh? What are you talking about?"

"Did she tell you that we kissed at Swinson's?"

I must've had the biggest smile I could possibly wear. Greg threw the book back in the locker.

"That *who* kissed?"

"Nicole and I. We're going out now."

He didn't smile or high-five me like I thought he would.

"*You* kissed Nicole?"

"Yeah."

"And she asked *you* out?"

"No, I asked her."

I felt like a badgered witness.

"And she said *yes*?"

"Yeah, what the fuck is your problem?"

"Well, you may want to let her and Wayne Decanter know about that. They've been making out in the gym all week."

Death punch!

"What?"

I choked back tears.

"Yep, saw them every friggin' day this week. They didn't see *me*, though."

Greg was angry when he said it because he wanted Nicole for himself, the bastard . . . and life was full of disappointments.

When I could no longer stand to re-watch—over and over again—the smut-laden projection in my head of that whore making out with blonde-haired, good-looking Wayne, I approached her like a red-faced madman. She didn't seem to follow, didn't understand my anger, like we'd never had our kiss. Even worse, she was wearing *our* purple flower in her hair. Wayne Decanter probably commented on it. Imposter! Nicole stared at me like I was crazy. She kept asking me what was wrong and why I was so upset.

"Swinson's?" I said. "Our kiss?"

"What kiss?"

What kiss?

Then the bell rang.

"I gotta go, Jake," she said, annoyed.

I was stunned as I walked to class.

I told Mrs. Drake that I wasn't feeling well, that I needed to go to the nurse.

"No," she said.

When that didn't work, I took more drastic measures to heighten my chances of an early exit from the grossly ordinary English lesson that she'd been regurgitating onto us, the students, receivers of such useless curriculum. I threw my book across the aisle, right at the back of Toby Waterfeld's stupid head, because, well, he was a dick, but mainly because I needed to get out of that classroom full of weirdos, pronto. And I'd figured if I was going down, I was going down pissing on someone I despised. Toby was a cliché, a bully, the unpopular bigger kid who already had facial hair, smelled like he didn't wipe his ass, and probably lived in a house full of anger and yelling, his father the perennial greenhorn car mechanic. He only picked on the smaller kids, the ones he knew he could strike fear into. I was small, but I wasn't one of his victims. I'm sure he'd be plotting some sort of revenge now.

I was promptly sent to the principal's office to escape the stench of subjects and predicates and adolescent lies. There my set chair would be waiting for me, my name stenciled on the back, *Jake Walden—Frequenter of the Office of the Principal*. I had to hurry, though. Mrs. Drake was so taken aback by my aggression that she'd failed to call down to the principal's office to notify them of my arrival. I sprinted, hoping her memory was no match for my world-class speed. When I arrived, sweaty and short of breath, I moaned and groaned to Principal Butler's secretary, Ms. Penny. She was reading the newspaper, didn't even bother to look up, scribbled on a hall pass, and handed it to me. I walked into the nurse's office without a knock.

"Well, hello," she said. "Not feeling well?"

I said nothing. I could only stare at her, hoping she would know how to make the pain go away.

"Come sit," she said.

I sat down on the cot and cried. She sat next to me, put her arm across my back, gently cupped my shoulder, and pulled me into the side of her breast. Her name was Ms. Lisa. She was beautiful.

MS. LISA

MS. LISA HAD midnight hair down to her breasts, tanned skin, and yellowy-green eyes that gleamed catlike through the windows of her simple black frames. Her face was soft and round, like Phoebe Cates. Something else I noticed . . . big tits, and shapely hips. Her accent was strange, not like the "wicked hahd" articulation of some of the other faculty members. She was from California.

I looked down at Ms. Lisa's other hand that rested on my lap, her fingertips ruby red. For a moment I thought she was going to kiss me. I would have let her. When she didn't, I felt sad again. She got up to open the curtain, the sun's rays bathing her lower thigh, just above the knee. She sat back down in a cold light-blue chair.

"Where does it hurt?" she asked with such understanding.

I didn't know what to say, couldn't stop staring.

"Is it your stomach?" she asked.

I shook my head, still teary-eyed. She placed her hand on my cheek, then my forehead.

"You don't feel warm, but let's go ahead and take your temperature anyway."

I enjoyed the cold, filmy texture of the thermometer, the way my teeth felt on the glass. I thought about biting it. As I patiently waited for the results, she smiled, her expression simpatico.

"Your temp is fine," she said. "You can stay for a bit, but I'll have to call your mom to let her know you're here."

She paused, I looked down at the floor, then she made a few vague comments about some boy who once broke her heart. I stopped crying and Ms. Lisa sent me on my way, never called my mother. I went home that day, crawled into my cubby, and thought about Ms. Lisa—still nothing came out. Later that night I wrote a song about her. It wasn't any good.

I started hanging around outside her office during my lunch period so I could accidentally bump into her, say hello, ask her how her day was going. She only turned me away a few times, when she was dealing with some snot-nosed faker. But mostly she'd invite me in, let me stay until I had to go to class. I wanted to stay there all day, escape the confines of academia, and wallow like any normal eleven-year-old who was dying by way of a girl. Ms. Lisa understood me. She'd been there, tasted the same theft of amour propre that resulted in the mutilated leftovers of a trampled heart, dripping through the fingers like a mangled tomato, lit on fire and stomped on like a bag of flaming bloody dog shit. Ms. Lisa was the perfect cure for my run-in with that red-eyed preteen she-devil. It wasn't long before I'd forgotten about Nicole and thought only of Ms. Lisa—her face, her legs, her breasts. I'd ask questions about her family in California.

"Do you miss them?" I asked.

"Very much," she said.

"Why don't you go visit?"

"I will soon, but I can't right now."

"Why not?"

"Oh, just tied up with a few things."

"What things?"

She smiled at my unstoppable—on the surface innocent—curiosity. I was more mature than she thought, but I let her think I was naive.

"Oh, let's just say I made a mistake."

"What kind of a mistake?"

"Do you know what divorce is?"

She went on to tell me all about her ex-husband—the reason she'd moved to Massachusetts—and how he cheated on her two weeks after they'd married. Her face sagged when she told the story. She moved all the way across the country just for him, and he took a shot at the first young, trampy waitress he set eyes on—a townie whore, she was. He was a real scumbag. I imagined pulling darts out of a stoked fire that painted the tips white-hot, then throwing them at his naked face. She didn't have any pictures of the Asshole at her desk. That's what she called him, the Asshole. His given name was Bart. Bart was originally from Texas. He didn't sound like much, and I could tell from her description that he was not anywhere near as fast as I was, on foot or on a bike. I pictured a fat-ass, lazy son of a bitch with stringy hair who came home from his job at the local bank and plopped down into his shit-brown leather recliner, cranking the handle back like it was the gear shift in his IROC-Z. The pig probably sat in his own farts all night, belting out unemotional orders for Bud Light and TV dinners. Microwaved Salisbury steak gravy mixed with mashed potatoes would drip down his patchy, bloated face, caking to his dirty mustache while he coated his already limited brain casing with the skank of episodic and psychotic programming. Only an idiot would succumb to such entrapment from the likes of Jerry Springer and Ricki Lake. I'd bet he'd never read a book in his life. My visits with Ms. Lisa were the highlight of every day . . . and then she was gone. I knocked on the door during lunch and a stranger waved me in.

"Who are you?" I asked.

"I'm Beatrice. Who are you, young man?"

"Well, where's Ms. Lisa?"

Beatrice went on to tell me that Ms. Lisa had moved back to California.

"I think she was from there, sweetheart, moved back to be with her—"

"Family," I said, interrupting. "Yeah, I know. Her mom's name is Elizabeth and she's sick. Ms. Lisa would have gone sooner had it not been for her son-of-a-bitch, asshole, cheating ex-husband," I continued, leaving Beatrice with wide eyes and an open mouth—terrible teeth.

I turned and walked out of the nurse's office and into the halls, watching the tiles pass with every step.

I can't believe she didn't say good-bye.

I tried to be understanding.

It would have been too hard for her to say good-bye. That's why she didn't. That must be why.

Ms. Lisa was fond of me, and the pain she would've felt from the fade in my gaze—had she told me of her plans—might have stopped her from leaving. But she had to go. Her mother *was* sick. And she probably needed to get away from the malodorous air surrounding her life, the gut-rot scent of the Asshole.

It's not like she met some other guy or anything. No way she could move on that quickly.

I figured that when I got a little bit older I would look her up, head out West, too. Maybe then we could make it work, pick up where we left off. Maybe she'd be waiting for me. I stopped going to the nurse's office after she left. There was this new girl in school, Jessica.

GREG DOGARD

BY SPRING I'D bent the truth enough in school to come off as interesting and cool. I was good at *pretending* to be confident. I knew I had a skill set, but didn't boast, and that magnified people's perception of me when I had a chance to show off said skills. If you're unexpectedly talented, people are drawn to you. The artful management of such behavioral distortion—on the surface—reeked of humble pie.

We were at Greg's house—me, Greg, Eric, and our other friend, Nick Patrick. Greg and I were fake fighting, just messing around while Nick and Eric were playing *The Legend of Zelda* on Greg's Nintendo. I was showing off some pretty good moves I'd picked up from the movie *Lone Wolf McQuade*—a Chuck Norris film. I pretended to be impressed with some of Greg's moves, played it up; none were that impressive. He asked if I'd taken karate before.

"A little bit. Not much," I said.

"Really? You seem like you know what you're doing," Greg said.

As he unknowingly slipped into my performance—now a crucial character in my story—I went in for the modest kill.

"Well, I don't want to brag too much."

"How long?"

"Few years."

"Like two?"

My facial disposition turned cold.

"Two and a half."

"What belt did you get to?"

"Got my black belt just before coming here."

The interior of the room changed. My claim got the attention of Eric and Nick as well.

"You're a black belt?" asked Nick.

"Bullshit!" said Eric.

I was naturally athletic, good at sports, anything physical. I was fast. I could jump really high, despite my being vertically challenged for my age—I was twelve years old and only four foot eight. I wasn't completely lying, though. I did earn an orange belt when I was ten years old. I was also a fan of martial arts movies—Chuck Norris and Bruce Lee were my favorites. I definitely had a black belt in martial-arts movie knowledge.

"I'm with Eric. I say bullshit," said Greg.

"You don't have to believe me," I said. "You wanna play video games or something?" I continued.

Greg contemplated.

"Prove it," he said.

"Nah, I don't wanna . . ."

"Don't wanna what?"

"I don't wanna hurt you."

Greg laughed nervously. I looked down at the floor to make sure there was a rug beneath him to break his fall. I really *didn't* want to hurt him at the time.

"All right, fine," I said as he kept egging.

"Show me whatcha got," Greg said.

Greg crouched into a sad excuse for a fighting stance—his hands were too low, feet too close together. The boy just didn't look the part. We settled in, plenty of space on all sides.

"Are you sure?" I said, reaffirming my position of chivalry.

"C'mon, Chuck Norris," said Greg.

I was flattered by the comparison even though I knew it was layered with sarcasm.

"Okay . . . Throw a kick," I said.

Greg fired off a sloppy side kick that I easily blocked with my left hand. Anyone could have. It was abysmal at best. Poor bastard was already panting from exhaustion.

"Higher," I said.

Greg threw his version of a roundhouse kick, not very good, too low and stiff as a board. But it was just high enough to cause his tan corduroys to stretch beyond their limitations, tearing open from knee to knee. While his dreadful leg sat poorly in the air, I dropped to the floor and accelerated my rotation one-hundred eighty degrees. My right heel clipped his flimsy stilts, sending him airborne. His hair stood tall, both legs now rising above his head, his torn pants exposing his tighty-whities. He looked pitiful. His arms flailed like a blind stork as he fell to the ground, laid out on his ass by a perfect leg sweep, incredibly executed. Sometimes I impressed myself. Greg came crashing down to the carpet with a dull thud that took the air out of him and shook the living room. Eric and Nick came scrambling over, not to check on Greg—who still lay flat on his back, filleted, staring at the ceiling—but to stare at me in awed silence. They'd never seen anything like it before, nor had Greg. After basking in the envy that shone bright on their faces, I bent down, self-righteous, to check on Greg. He tilted his head forward, planting his chin on his chest, looking both impressed and happy to be alive.

"You okay?" I asked.

"Holy shit, dude . . ." he said after I pulled him up from his back to a sitting position. "That was awesome," he continued.

"Thanks," I said.

"Man, you weren't kidding."

"Nope."

"What the hell was that?" asked Eric, clearly annoyed by my showcase.

He didn't seem to appreciate my fine art as much as Greg and Nick. He never did like it much when others got the attention. Up until then I think Eric thought he had one over on me—my being the new kid and all. Now, he saw that I could do something that he couldn't.

"Leg sweep," I said.

My tone was intentional. I looked only at Eric, the way one poker player looks at another as he waits for him to go all in.

"He's a friggin' black belt," said Greg.

Eric tried to look unimpressed.

"That was awesome," added Nick.

That's about the length of Nick's articulation, but he was correct in his analysis. He was harmless and all, just typically at a loss for words.

"Whatever. I'm getting something to eat," Eric said.

Eric walked into the kitchen. While he pouted, I secured the position of my new disciples by showing Nick and Greg a few moves that I knew were easy for them to handle—like how to break a guy's thumb with a handshake. I'd seen it in a Kung Fu magazine. Eric was brooding over by the fridge, leaning on its open door, staring at nothing as he tried to overhear our conversation. He peeked over, couldn't help himself. I looked back, equipped with the grin of a warden to an inmate. The jealous bastard turned away from the fridge and hunched down at the kitchen table with a container of strawberry yogurt he was never going to eat.

Later on that day we went skateboarding at Swinson's, on the tennis courts. Eric pouted the whole time, said he had to go home; the day wasn't going his way. Nick went home, too. Greg and I went back to his house for some snacks. Mrs. Dogard, Greg's mom, walked in while we were eating Frosted Flakes out of the box and noticed the artwork on the grip tape of my board, a swastika drawn in with a permanent marker. That symbol, of course, would be forever marred by a world-class asshole who made it synonymous with genocide. Mrs. Dogard was Jewish.

"What is that?" she asked sternly.

"What is what?" I asked back.

"That"—she pointed—"on your skateboard . . ." She walked over, scraped her finger over the grip tape, leaving small white flakes of flesh. "I'm talking about *that* right there," she continued.

"Oh, that. It's just something I've seen other skaters put on their boards. Why?"

I had an aversion to toeing the line, doing things in the presumed order of "the people." I often chose an alternate route, feeding on the reaction, especially when I knew the facts. I'd done my research on the cause of Mrs. Dogard's discontent. That's why I put it there, for the confrontations, just so I could prove someone wrong. It wasn't as if I agreed with a guy who incinerated millions of people because he didn't like their hair color—I did not. My mother never noticed it.

"You don't know what that is?" she asked in awe of my perceived naivety. "Yet you still painted it on your board?"

"I didn't paint it, I used a marker."

I made an insensitive scribbling motion with my hand.

"Mom, come on," Greg chimed in, embarrassed at her line of questioning.

I understood her asking. She should have been offended; she didn't know the true origin of the symbol.

"It's okay," I said to Greg, my eyes still on his mother.

"What does it mean?" I asked.

"It's a swastika . . . as in Adolf Hitler . . . as in the leader of the Germans in World War II. Killed millions. Does your mother know that you have that?"

Her lordly sarcasm was massive. That was fine but she was too close, about a foot away from my face. I could smell her—her breath, her hair, her body odor.

"No, Sharon. Mom hasn't noticed," I said calmly.

She backed up. Greg didn't notice, but Sharon did—the need to be more careful. I appreciated her newfound respect, so I reengaged . . . under the new regime.

"I know who Hitler is. But that's not why I put it there. That *symbol* is the ancient symbol of auspiciousness in Hinduism, Buddhism, and Jainism. Did you know that, Sharon?"

Greg was frozen.

"Well . . . that may be . . . but . . . well . . . it's also something that the Nazis used . . . and . . . well, he was the worst of the worst and I think you should consider removing it."

I looked at Greg. His eyes begged my pardon.

"Sure thing, Mrs. Dogard. My apologies. I didn't mean to offend you. I'll take it off right away. Do you have a black marker?"

Right there in Mrs. Dogard's kitchen, I covered the offensive symbol. When I went home, I drew in a new one, on the underside of my board. The old one was fading anyway. I went back to Greg's later that night and stuck a screwdriver through one of Mrs. Dogard's tires. Because fuck her, that's why. And fuck Greg, too . . . and Rene Teller, for that matter. She ended up being my girlfriend junior year. Long story short, there was a class ski trip. I didn't go. Rene and Greg went. Before the trip,

Rene was my girlfriend and Greg was my best friend. After the trip, Rene was no longer my girlfriend and Greg was dead to me.

OBJECTS IN THE MIRROR

BY SENIOR YEAR I was angry as hell, an ungrateful, entitled teenage asshole. Mom had been helping me with my college applications. Actually, she'd buttoned up all the drudge to that point. I wanted nothing to do with college or anything that wasn't cloaking me in some semblance of immediate gratification, like playing guitar or getting fucked up.

"Can you come sign this, hon?" Mom asked.

"Why don't you just sign it, Mom? I don't even know if I want to go to college," I yelled from upstairs.

"What, sweetie?"

I was on my way out to hang with a few delinquents similar to myself, some guys I was jamming with—they were in possession of some brilliant painkillers. I stomped downstairs and into the dining room.

"Can you please just sign it for me? I'm so sick of dealing with this shit, Ma. I feel like I sign something or have to read something about college every day."

A complete disregard for her feelings, for her efforts, for the countless hours she'd spent penning those lifeless forms so that her son would have a chance at an education. I quickly regretted my lash of insensitivity. Hurting my mother's feelings was not my strong suit. She's the one person in the world who was supposed to be exempt from the swollen sting of my random acts of cruelty. I wouldn't let anyone hurt her (that was supposed to include myself).

Mom's lack of oral response and sullen head drop, at first, were far worse than anything she could have verbally laced up and hurled in my direction.

"I'm sorry, Mom, I didn't mean that. I do appre—"

She started to cry, so I went over to console her, but she stopped me cold with the truth of her wounds, hitting me hard with a guilt-laced bell ringer.

"I just . . . I just feel like you don't appreciate all of the work that I'm putting into this for you, Jake. College is important," she said.

I tried to backpedal, but her tears grew bigger, killing me on the inside with the poison in her pain.

"Mom, I do appre—"

"You used to be such a sweet kid, and now . . . now you're just so . . . goddamn mean. What happened to you?"

Death punch!

Her sadness, united with the stone axiom of her verbal daggers—that I was turning into an unappreciative little monster and breaking her heart—created a fireball of guilt inside of me. That guilt turned to anger, and before she could puncture my heart any more with her truth, I let the rage out of the cage, turning to my right in a spell of ferocity, releasing a house-shaking roar as I smashed the wall with my left hand, creating a crater twice the size of my fist. My mother's face froze, the look more disappointment than fear. Her tears spit through her hands as she covered her eyes to avoid contact with mine. Stan leapt from his recliner in the living room—he was reading something, probably historical nonfiction. His book went flying into the air. He wasn't angry, just startled and concerned about the ruckus and the roar. Stan sympathized with me much of the time. My mother had a tendency to ride me pretty hard when it came to, well, everything—school, friends, sports—but it was only because she wanted what was best for me. She wasn't as hard on my older brother, Andrew. Mom let him get away with more and she paid for it with a few trips to the police station—minor stuff, but still. She's an over-reactor. And, like myself, there was no middle of the road with her; it was either extreme this way or extreme that way, and she wanted me to excel at school and at sports, to surround myself with good people, and to basically not make any mistakes whatsoever. I didn't exactly follow the plan. We were like two rams smashing heads for most of my teenage years.

I cocked my arm back to lay another hole in the light-blue drywall when Stan caught me with his words of wisdom.

"Yeah, go ahead, put another hole in the wall, why don't ya. A lotta good that's gonna do," he said, loudly.

Stan was, in the main, a reserved guy, but he'd walked in on a situation where I was punching the wall and my mother was crying her eyes out—it warranted a reaction. Stan loved my mother and was seamlessly loyal to her. It's one of the qualities within him that I admired most. We'd all come up roses when he gained entry into our lives. I agreed with what Stan said, but I wasn't about to admit it. Instead, I withheld a second punch and ripped open the front door, growling like a spoiled child on my way out. I jumped into my black 1987 Mustang convertible—passed down from my brother, who'd moved to Chicago to trade stocks—and peeled off fast and loose down my street, no doubt warranting a future phone call to my parents from our pissed-off neighbors.

"Your sons drive like reckless assholes," they'd shout through the receiver. "We've got kids, for chrissake."

My foot laid heavy to the floor; one would have thought I was in the Daytona 500 rearing up for the pole position as I passed car after car with shrewd precision. I didn't take my foot off the gas. The street signs and the buildings that I left in my path seemed to pull away, melting in fear at the vibrations of my automotive tirade. Bystanders out walking their dogs stopped and stared. Some would yell, some would wince in fear, some shook their heads in disgust. *Punk kid*, they thought. They were right. My gas tank, unlike my fury, was near empty. I jerked the wheel to the right, pulling into one of the mom-and-pop gas drops. One of the cars I'd passed—a gray Saab station wagon—clocked my sharp detour and followed, pulling up next to the tank behind me. When I turned the car off, extinguishing my tantrum, my eyes began to fill. I watched my driver's-side mirror bring the angry motorist closer. There were a lot of tough people in my town, so you just never knew what was going to happen. This guy was maybe thirty-five, about five ten, average build, scruffy and rugged in his Red Sox hat and dark-blue puffy jacket—it was January in New England.

I can take this guy.

I wiped what was about to be the tears from my eyes and prepared to tell him to fuck off—chances were he wasn't coming over to pay me compliments for my near perfect performance of urban vehicular slalom. I rolled down my window as he approached, propping myself upright for a confrontation that I wasn't ready for. I could see the down-talking condescension already leaking from his trap.

"You little shit, what the fuck do you think you're d—"

The angry man took one look at my clammy, sad, red face and became the father that he probably already was, who'd decided that this sullen young man who was trying his hardest not to cry—someone's child—was longing for a touch of leniency, some semblance of sympathy, an ounce of empathy . . .

because life can be a blank fucking map sometimes. He was no longer the angry driver who thought some punk kid was being disrespectful, passing him on a local side street at such a high speed. He changed so fast, almost the second we made eye contact. I reminded him of the young man that *he* used to be, a lost teenager who'd made mistakes, acted carelessly. Maybe, like me, he just wanted to grab hold of it once again—that love and loyalty that he'd entered the world knowing—in its unconditional state, to prove that it was real, that it still existed. At that, the kind man understood me more than *I* understood me. He stared at me with his all-knowing eyes, a relenting gaze, as my posture collapsed from emotional exhaustion.

"Are—ahh . . . are you okay, buddy?" he asked.

I looked down at my steering wheel. I was embarrassed about what I'd done, ripping across the potholed concrete, endangering society.

"I'm sorry," I said. "I'm really sorry."

It's all I could muster as I began to cry. There were no more words that I could give him, and the forgiving man sensed that I needed to be left alone, honoring my regret. I was taken by his reaction, his demeanor, his comforting posture—like he was giving me advice without as much as a word. He'd been in my shoes, and so he ceased judgment. Perhaps he remembered a time where—out of fear, out of anger—he, too, had sped off from his home, unable to control his emotions, distraught at the resulting person that he'd become, stuck inside a bottle of anger. Whatever his past might have been, at that moment, he was just a man, and he saw that I was just a boy.

When I left the gas station, I went over to my friend's house, pounded a few beers, and took two Tylox. All I had to do was take a few pills, and the pain, it withered away. Shortcuts are the footfall to all that is dangerous, but life is a hell of a lot easier that way.

11:23 PM – AUGUST 13

THE CROWD AT the Whisky was raucous for such a small venue. Although we still haven't signed on any dotted lines, we've amassed—through task and talent—a substantial fan base; we're an adroit bunch. It's taken a little bit of luck and a magnitude of skill-honing hard work to finally harvest interest from major record labels. I'd gotten word earlier in the week that Epic, Sony, and Interscope would be appraising the twilight's endowment—namely us. Reps from each of the labels called me directly. I doubled as our booking agent, went by the moniker Brent Ashby.

Clive popped his head backstage.

"Hey," he said.

"What's up, asshole? We go on in like thirty seconds," I said.

"Alison's here."

"You're shitting me?"

"*No, I will not shit on you* . . . Dude, stop asking me to shit on you. It makes me uncomfortable."

I flipped him off and turned to look for a response from my bandmates. They were too busy jostling with knobs and pedals to notice that Clive was even present.

"Who's she here with?" I asked.

"That British guy . . . what's his name . . . Wears tight pants . . . looks like a fucking ThunderCat."

I rolled my eyes as he continued.

"They have that song you like to jerk off to . . . 'Man Hammock' or some shit . . . Peebo Man-cream . . ."

Clive was great at making light of a situation—i.e., the verbal hammers—a master of not only creating tension but alleviating it. He knew how I felt about Alison. He knew this could be potentially incendiary to my performance.

"Penro? Penro Mindcat?" I asked.

"Yeah, that chick . . . looks more like a Penelope, though."

Penro Mindcat was the lead singer for WutzIsName, a platinum rock band from London—Zeppelin meets Elton John. I'd heard stories about him, that he was a fucking nutter. He once fixed himself atop the Chateau Marmont Hotel after selling out the Hollywood Bowl. Drunk on his own personal status, the crazy Brit hurled self-important diatribes to the civilians below while brandishing a twelve-inch blade that kissed the pruned crust of his nut sack. He kept threatening to let his balls fall to the ground as a show of benevolence to his adoring fans.

"The fuck do I care?" he said. "I've got everything. I'll buy new balls."

Aside from all that, he's a talented songwriter. The band had recently released their umpteenth hit single, "You Don't Gotta Go Home but You Can't Stay Here." They're in their last act, but plenty relevant, remaining passionate in their poetic motives. It's their argument that attracts me; some lyrics resonate.

It is only until that within the tin of the dawn bursts open
Just before the middle hours of our lives
That we realize the beginning hours of our true selves
Free from disguise

So don't you think you know
Don't you tell me so
What lies behind my eyes

Despite Penro's highfalutin personality, I do appreciate his fuck-all attitude and lyrical prose.

I stepped back, took a moment. I couldn't care less about Penro, that pompous, uppity Brit. I was fine with the fact that the world's most notorious front man was about to pay witness to our band's annihilation of the stage. Alison, though, she'd stung me something fierce, and she'd led him here for a reason, to get under my skin.

Or maybe she's here to get me back.

Things hadn't ended well with Alison. I hadn't wanted them to end at all. I loved her . . . I still do. A sensuous young beauty from Denmark—light-brown hair, caramel skin, and crystal eyes of the ocean's blue. I was hit right away when I met her, as soon as she opened her mouth. It wasn't what she said. It was the way she folded her bottom lip at the end of her words, pinching it beneath her upper ivories. She'd bite down almost to the point of puncture, favoring one side, creating a welcomed disturbance inside of me. We'd met at a party in my apartment building on Yucca seven months ago. It would be the genesis of an incredible five weeks full of sexual diagnostics abounding with role playing, cocaine and ecstasy, loads of Viagra, and some girl named Sally from Copenhagen making an appearance at intervals. And then it wasn't.

"How's she look?" I asked Clive backstage.

"Who, Penelope?"

"Alison, dickhead! You know Penro's got more hit songs than fucking Lionel Richie, right?"

"Whatever. She looks pretty fuckin' hot."

I pictured her biting her lip.

"Of course she does." I imagined fucking her. "All right, mate. See you after the show."

"Hey, how come you never let her blow me? I thought we were friends, bitch."

"Hey, how come you keep eating Twinkies, you fat fuck?"

I gave him the finger. Clive grinned.

"Why don't you go see if Penro will blow you? He's a liberal rock-and-roll Brit. Might even let you call him Penelope if you ask real pretty," I said.

He laughed, shifted gears, and dug into Tim.

"Hey, Tim, can you go easy on the gay guitar faces tonight? Makes my pants feel weird."

I laughed, turned toward Tim; he looked at me. Clive's sinister laugh trailed off and he was gone.

A voice came over the speakers—Mike, the sound guy.

"Ladies and gentlemen . . . please welcome . . . When the Lion Came."

Show time!

I love it here!

I hate it here!

I could taste it on the tip of my inventive tongue, the urge to make tonight's cavalcade monumental, the best damn administration of rock-and-roll prowess I'd ever aroused, a revenant piece of artistry.

Don't look at her.

I started in with the intro to "Batshit Crazy"—a song about a girl. The curtains came up. The smell of all the liquor in the world hit fast. My gut went hollow, like it does right before liftoff. I could feel the hairs on my arms standing in ovation at the size of the crowd.

My back was turned toward them . . .

The lights went up . . .

The roar of the crowd . . .

Hector's deep kick . . .

Tim's bass line warm and in check . . .

Avi's building, rhythmic ax tone digging into the subaqueous earth of rock and roll . . .

My turn now. Don't look at her. Look at the crowd, not her. Ready . . . ready . . .

I turned around.

Fuck, she looks beautiful.

Why do you make me batshit crazy
You never woke me, just upped and left me
That hateful, wasted, hack drug dealer
Got in your head, told you I can't heal ya
Took my wallet, took my car and drove
Off to his house for another bloody nose
A broken face we can mend
But your betrayal has no end
Never thought it'd phase me, but
You drive me batshit crazy

ALISON PIERSON

SOMEWHERE WITHIN THE libidinous fog of our vulgar jamboree, at the heel of a four-day, epic sex-capade in my apartment, Alison snatched three hundred dollars from my dresser and went AWOL for two days with my car. One of her roommates, Sally from Copenhagen, was still there, but she wasn't really my brand to loiter with in solitary. I did let her blow me once while Alison was gone, but it was more like twiddling thumbs in the hedonic interim. I kept picturing Alison bent over in the back seat of my car getting plowed something awful by her ex-boyfriend. I could hardly keep my erection in Sally's mouth, even with the aid of a boner pill.

I paced, hanging on tenterhooks for her return. I picked up my guitar, played "Texas Flood" by Stevie Ray Vaughan angrily till my fingers bled, then sat on the floor, back against the wall, gnawing on my fingernails, smearing blood across my bottom lip, staring intently at the door while Sally flipped through the channels.

"Just call her," said Sally.

I called and called. Alison never answered.

"She does this," said Sally.

"Does what?" I asked.

"Disappears. Makes boys angry."

"I'm not angry."

Sally shrugged.

"Are you gonna keep fucking flipping through channels?" I asked.

She did.

Alison opened the door ten minutes later. I exploded off the floor, a madman, disheveled and greasy haired, wearing only the bottoms of my red-and-black-checkered flannel pj's. She was off-balance wasted, played the role of indifferent-to-her actions flawlessly, uniform to an Academy Award–winning contessa. She said she went to buy more drugs from some guy who she knew. I knew what that meant. I knew who she'd gone to see—Roger.

Roger is her ex-boyfriend, deals pills, X, blow; she met him at Las Palmas. Alison and her vampy foreign cohorts would frequent the popular night club where Roger and his friends amassed; they'd dance, drop X, fuck. Their relationship ended violently. He gave her a black eye, bloody nose. She never told me why. This, I found out later, was a week after we met, the same day Clive overdosed. I wanted to kill Roger. Violently was how I pictured it, but Alison made me promise to stay away.

Alison closed the door, stood there draped in a long, khaki-colored trench coat—a man's coat. I caught the shine of sparkling metallic purple, a bikini she wore underneath. I tugged at the knotted belt to sharpen the view. Her tits were perfect, so real, so rare. I felt a growth in my flannel jammies. In the midst of my green-eyed rage, I was still enamored by her beauty, her symmetry, her lusty tableau.

We are who we are.

Her pepper-red lipstick was smeared off to the left side of her face, the under part of her eyes plastered with the drippy remnants of mascara running away from her crystal blues, and her hair was a tangled mop. She looked like a sex worker, a two-timing Danish harlot after a forty-eight-hour shift. I leaned in. She pulled back.

"*Where the fuck have you been?*" I screamed.

She looked right through me.

"What the fuck, dude? Why are you screaming?" she asked.

"Dude? Dude? Because you took three hundred bucks from my fucking dresser . . . and stole my car . . . *dude*. You've been gone for fuckin' two days, Alison!"

"Relax. I went to this guy's house, a friend, to get some more coke," she said.

"Some guy? You mean, Roger . . . as in the guy you used to fuck, Roger? The same guy that punched you in the fucking face, Roger?"

"What? No! I wasn't even gone that long, Jake."

She sat on the floor.

"You were gone for two days, Alison. Where are the fucking drugs?"

I might have forgiven her had she come back with something to numb the pain. Then we could get high and keep having sex, never to traverse the outside world again. But . . .

"My friend, he didn't have many . . . any," she said, laughing.

"What's so fucking funny? And where's my fucking money?"

She pulled sixty-five bucks and some change out of her trench coat.

"Where's the rest?"

Sally started gathering her things.

"My roommate. She needed money for bills."

"I thought Sally was your roommate."

"Penny. My other roommate. I went to my place to get clothes. She needed like two hundred something for bills."

"You paid your *bills* with my money?"

"It was past due. She was freaking out. I'll pay you back, I promise."

"And the coat?"

"Oh, yeah, I saw it at a thrift store on my way back, was like twenty bucks. It's cool, right?"

"Are you fucking kidding me? You've been gone for fucking two days, with my fucking car and my fucking three hundred dollars, both of which you took without asking. You not only decided to pay your fucking bills with *my* money, but you also went shopping? For a coat? For what? 'Cause it's cold outside?"

"Yeah, it was cold."

"Well, maybe next time you don't walk around wearing a fucking bikini when you're not at the beach. You gonna wear snow boots to a pool party? Did you go to the store like that?"

She was starting to fade.

"All my clothes were dirty."

"You went to Roger's, didn't you?"

She shook her head in disgust.

"Don't fucking lie to me, Alison. You get high and fuck him?"

"You don't know what you're saying, Jake. I wasn't even gone for that lo—"

"*Two days, Alison! You were gone for two fucking days* . . . and I know you had sex with that motherfucker."

"Fuck you, Jake!"

Alison got up as Sally was on her way out. They opened the door and left.

"We're not done here."

"You're not my fucking boyfriend, Jake."

Death punch!

My heart dropped like a blood-soaked sponge, leaving an immediate puddle upon its doughy splatter.

Why could I not see this coming? She doesn't love me. Where the fuck is Clive?

I continued yelling at the door, still fit to be tied, maddened and beet-red from the buckshot of Alison's disloyal pose. I grabbed the chair that rested in the corner by the door. My body shook. The veins in my arms grew into rooted lines, pulsating up through the skin. I choked the back of the chair as tightly as I could and hurled it against the wall as I let out a graveled roar—the terra firma bubbling in my chest. The chair shattered into splintered woe, collateral damage. I caught my reflection in the closet mirror—the biggest eyes I'd ever seen.

Is that me?

I went for the lava lamp across the room; it sat on the sill of the window I'd forgotten to close. All of Yucca Street must have heard my devil cries.

I wonder if my new neighbor, Honey, heard me.

I grabbed the lamp with both hands, a dual slap on cooled glass, hurled it across the room, painting the pale wall an angry red. Clive burst through the door, guns blazing, primed to deliver fists at the mask of any sorry motherfuckers who might have motivated me to lose my cool. I turned in reaction, not knowing who it was at first, ready to pounce, my hands up in front of my face as he always reminded me to do. My breath was heavy, my chest doubled in size. But *I* was the only villain in the room. We both loosened our dispositions, looked down at the mess.

"What up, boy?" he said, so oddly calm.

He walked over to the bedroom window, closed it, and sat on the bed. My hands dangled by my sides, hanging like fifty-pound weights. I stared at the shrapnel on the floor, afraid of what I'd done, but couldn't help but feel the power of it, the comfort. Such dynamism!

I could get addicted to such a feeling.

"You all right?" asked Clive.

"Yut," I said.

"You got blood on your lip."

"Yut."

It was silent for a time. He waited patiently.

"Wanna grab a bite?" I asked.

Clive responded in stride.

"Yut . . . and a beer," he said.

In a flash, he was gone. The door was open, and a small green pill rested on the table near it. I popped it in my mouth, threw on a pair of black high-top Chucks, changed my shirt, and grabbed my Sox hat. I turned on the bathroom light out of habit, then off again just as fast, didn't like what I saw. I released my breath and grabbed my Elvis shades—a place to hide. I brushed my off-whites in the half dark, staring down at the lonely running water, the only sound in the room. Clive was waiting for me at the front door wearing sunglasses and a blue fitted Red Sox hat turned backward. In rhythm, he bore passage to the hall like a chauffeur opening the car door. I walked through first. Clive followed behind.

"That was my fucking lava lamp, asshole," he said.

He never let me drown.

11:28 PM – AUGUST 13

ALISON STOOD STILL in the audience. That concave dip between her neck and chest glistened with a shallow pool of sweat, pumping through the surface of her skin. I couldn't smell her, but I did anyway, because I remembered. Her hair was the same. Her smile was the same. Her eyes were more blue than the day we were through; they were crystal again. She looked at me the way she had the first time. She'd never seen me perform. Such a power to hold. I could almost hear the drip hit the floor, falling from high atop her inner thigh.

The crowd was in. Penro was sold. The record execs (they wore suits) were standing stoically next to the A&R guys (they weren't wearing suits). The young men who cared about music watched *us*; they moved, they smiled. The old men who cared only about dollars and cents and sex with whores behind closed doors, they watched the crowd; their faces didn't change, not once. *Can we sell these guys, make most of the money?* they thought.

Clive stood in the back of the house, alone. The song ended. I thanked everyone for coming out.

"Ladies and gentlemen, Mr. Penro Mindcat from WutzIsName," I said, pointing to the rock god, intentionally nonchalant. "We are gathered in the presence of greatness. Thanks for coming out, man."

He nodded and waved. I took a sip of whiskey from a glass. Alison whispered something in his ear, then headed to the bar. She sat next to Clive. They didn't realize they were next to each other. They'd only met one other time. At the opposite end of the bar were Peter and Ray; I'm pretty sure it was them. I'd reached the part of the show when I felt just fine about myself. The anxiety had leveled off, skirting the path of turbulent truth that would find me in the morning. Here I could pretend that life was grand. Here I was comfortable. Drugs and booze helped. That and the energy I'd ejaculated onto the stage, hate fucking all that burned. We played a few more songs, closed it out with "Under the Rug"—the title of our album. I sat down at the piano. My fingers fell to the keys like a feather to the earth, resulting in a sound that fumed from the grand like a last dying breath. Such sullen chords drew color from the faces of our covey's gathered company, the melody leaving no room for light of any kind.

Why did he never get what was coming to him
The lion came, put his hand upon my head
Why was my innocence not worth salvaging
When the lion came, I thought that I was dead
You never asked again
He never met the judge
You all tried to pretend
Then you swept it under the rug

12:01 AM – AUGUST 14

I WALKED BACKSTAGE ready for more cocaine. When I'm down, I need drugs. When I'm elated, I want drugs. I never really enjoyed life quite as much in the absence of such things. Living clean could be boring and hellish. I forgot Clive had the blow, so I settled for a blast of Jim Beam on the rocks, then out to meet and greet. The label people pounced as soon as we hit the bar. They said we'd be famous, said we'd sell millions (*yank! yank!*), bought drinks, promised there'd be sunshine—we'd heard it all before, done a few showcases for some major labels a year ago, but to no avail. They all said the same shit. I saw their faces, heard their voices. But all I could think about was that Clive had our remedy. Usually, he meets me backstage. In the midst of many agreeable nods and searches for Clive, I noticed Alison heading my way.

"Hey, Jake," she said.

I wanted to look her in the eye and tell her what I really thought: that I fucking loved her, that I fucking hated her, that I wanted to fuck her, that I wanted her to fuck off.

"Hey," I said.

"That was an incredible show, Jake . . . really . . . So good. Penro was impressed," she continued, searching for the right things to say but failing.

Is she fucking serious?

"Yeah, thanks," I said.

Then it was quiet, our eyes avoiding each other's.

"New boyfriend?" I asked.

"No . . . just hanging out," she said, biting her lip the way she does.

I imagined her and Penro fucking, made me hard.

It's not serious, I know it.

"What happened to Roger?"

"Roger? Jesus, Jake. Not that again. I'm not with him, not after what he did. I told you this before."

I skipped past it.

"Right. So . . . you liked the show, huh?"

"Yeah, I did. You're so talented, Jake. Honestly, I had no idea."

"Well, you never gave me a chance to show you, now, did you?"

She began to apologize. I interrupted. Part of me felt bad. Part of me felt like I had been a bit of a psychopath that night in my apartment. Part of me was thinking that maybe Alison and I could try again. With her, I was equal parts happy and sad, simultaneously wanted and needy. We had all the elements for a bad ending . . . but I didn't care.

"You know what . . . don't sweat it, seriously. It's fine . . . really. I was way out of line. We were both pretty fucked up," I said.

"Yeah, we were. But it was fun, though . . . us, I mean. We had fun," she said.

"It was. We did."

We went back and forth for a bit, catching up. She told me she was lonely here in Hollywood. I sympathized. Hollywood could be a friendless pit. Sally from Copenhagen had gone back to . . . well . . . Copenhagen, I guess, and Alison's *new* roommate was a recluse.

"She literally never speaks," she said.

I didn't tell her how much I missed her. I didn't tell her that things hadn't been so great lately. She told me she met Penro backstage when his band played at the Hollywood Bowl about a month ago. I pretended that I didn't care.

"Are you seeing anyone?" she asked.

"Nothing serious," I said. "Hey, have you seen Clive?"

"Who?"

"Clive."

"But I thoug—"

Penro burst into the conversation, rambling erratically in his eccentric British tongue. The accent was slightly exaggerated, if you ask me.

"Holy fucking shit, mate . . . *that* . . . was a fantastic show," he said.

His jaw rocked like a boat on the high seas and his eyes were as big as two moons.

"Thanks, mate. Glad you enjoyed it," I said.

"I mean it, one of the best I've seen in a long time, man. Reminds me of our early days, ya know?" he said, staring, reminiscing.

Penro turned to Alison.

"Oh, hey, sweetheart. You two know each other?" he asked.

Alison looked at me. I looked at her with not quite a smile. *Better than you ever will.*

"Yeah, we know each other pretty well," I said.

"Cool, cool, all right, well, listen, mate, I want to invite you and your band back to my glorious mansion to do loads of cocaine off the tits and asses of lovely naked women—no offense, love—and drink four-hundred-dollar bottles of champagne until our livers shrink and our balls shrivel into nothingness," he said. "Let's go, whataya say? C'mon, man, you're a star now. *Everyone's* gonna want to fuck you, mate."

I looked at Alison. Alison looked at me.

"Yeah, man. What's the address?" I asked.

"Fuckin' 'ell, mate, you'll come with me. I've a bloody driver."

I told him I'd meet him outside in ten minutes, then went looking for Clive. I checked the bathroom to see if he was blowing lines. I was surrounded by black walls, dirty stalls, and the stench of drunk ejaculate. I reached into my left jacket pocket for a smoke and found the rest of the cocaine from earlier. Clive must have slipped it in there for me. I went into the last stall for a key bump.

"Hey . . ."

Clive!

"I'm in here," I said.

I came out of the stall offering Clive the bag.

"I'm okay right now, brother," he said.

Huh?

"Everything all right?"

"Yut."

"Hey, Penro just invited us to his house in the hills. He's throwing a full-on British-style rock-and-roll party. Cocaine, titties, champagne. Let's hit it."

"Naw, you go ahead. I think I'll call it a night."

"No? The fuck is wrong with you?"

"All good, brother. I just think it's time for me to go. This is *your* night. You did good, Jake. Looks like the record labels are into it. I'm proud of you, brother."

I was riding pretty high from the show, so I moved past the phenomenon of Clive *not* wanting to finish out the night. I thanked him with a hug, told him I'd see him later, and walked away. Before I left . . .

"What it look like!"

"What it is!"

I hitched a ride in Penro's limo. Rex, the head of A&R from Sony, and a couple guys from Interscope who Penro knew came with us. Penro's bodyguard, Leon, was there as well. I was sitting opposite Penro and Alison, next to the label guys. They were all jockeying for position while Penro leaned in to say something to Leon, asking him to call someone. Roger, I think he said.

Alison's Roger?

Alison watched me the whole ride while I talked shop.

She wants me back. She at least wants to fuck.

We pulled up to Penro's palace in the hills of Hollywood, a dimly lit ostentation on the bluff. The driveway was already full so we took a spot in the back. As soon as we got out of the limo, Penro, Leon, and the label guys went for the back door. Alison and I stayed behind. No one noticed and she grabbed my hand.

"Follow me," she said.

"What about your boyfriend?" I asked.

"He's not my boyfriend, Jake."

That sounds familiar.

She walked me down some stairs to where the guest house was. It was dark and empty and secluded from the main quarters. She lifted a flowerpot and pulled out a key to unlock the door. We went at it as soon as we cracked the threshold. She stuck her hand down my pants. I swelled.

"I miss you, Jake," she said in between tongues.

I concurred while pulling her silk sleeveless black blouse over her head. She wasn't wearing a bra. Her tits were perfect, tanner than usual. Her miniskirt was quick to follow her blouse, descending into the darkness on the other side of the sofa. I wet my finger and rubbed her clit. I was rude to it. We stumbled into some furniture, knocked over a few accessories, not caring where we ended up. She yanked my shirt off as we fell to the floor, landing on a rug that felt more like a bed. Even with all the cocaine I'd done that evening, my hard-on raged. Off came my pants, then her panties. I was getting ready to put it in. But I had to know.

"Did you go to Roger's that night?" I asked.

"Jake, no way. You know what he did to me. I would never," she said. "I went to see this guy from Denmark to get some more drugs."

I was relieved.

"I should have fucked him up for what he did to you," I said, referring back to Roger.

"No, Jake, he's a really dangerous guy. He's done some fucked-up things. Not just what he did to me, but with other people, too."

"Like what?"

She was reluctant.

"Tell me," I said.

"Like he has a stash of bad drugs that he gives to people who fuck with him. What do you call it . . . a bad batch . . ."

"What the fuck!"

Alison went on to tell me about how Roger gave bad drugs to a guy that he'd found out was selling in his territory. The guy was undercutting Roger's prices. Some hippy, new in town, had no idea what he was getting into. All Roger really had to do was flash a gun, scare the guy off, and that would have been that. Instead, Roger invited the guy to his apartment to discuss working together, offered the poor bastard a sample of the goods, and then watched as he convulsed on the floor. When I asked Alison how she knew this, she looked down at the floor.

"Because . . . I was there," she said.

"What happened to the guy?"

"I don't know. Roger told me to leave. Said to keep my mouth shut about what I saw."

"Motherfucker . . ."

"Please . . . just stay away from him, Jake . . . Please."

She kissed me, then lowered her head to take me in her mouth. All I could think about now was ingrown toenails and burning corpses. You know, to keep from coming too quickly. Don't judge.

Afterward we shared a cigarette, still naked on the carpet, staring up at the high ceilings in Penro's guest house.

"I love fucking you," I said.

"I love fucking you, too," she said.

I had to kiss her again.

"How much longer do you have in the States?"

"Few more weeks."

"Visa run out?"

"Yeah . . . and I'm not married, so . . ."

She looked beautiful and I didn't want her to go.

"I'll marr—"

There was an interruption of voices outside the front door. We gathered our clothes and left through the slider. Entering the main house through the back door, we were hit with the turbulence of a true-to-form rock-and-roll Hollywood Hills rage. The Who's "Tommy" danced across the ceiling of a kitchen made of stone. Clothing the frames of the party's seedy lepers were leather and jean, silk and velvet, cotton T-shirts and see-through lace. All looked as if they had been there before, in a place they all thought they belonged. To the left was a colossal aquarium that housed a fifteen-foot boa constrictor, the lead act for the soulless party people who gathered around to witness its devouring of an innocent guinea pig. The giant snake was calculatedly philosophic as the guinea pig was lowered into the tank, made to immediately suffer through the anticipation of its own horrible death. The snake knew that it was in control and it tortured the frightened critter by simply waiting, forcing the rodent to taste the drip of death before the grip tightened and the lights went out. I was short of breath and my body tightened with dreaded anticipation.

"Just fucking do it already!" I shouted, unaware that my internal thought had escaped the confines of my mouth.

Alison was startled by the verbal explosion but the look in her eyes was sympathetic. The barbaric audience rubbernecked in my direction, probably expecting a laugh or sarcastic grin instead of the anger and compassion that lit up my display.

"What the fuck is wrong with you people?" I shouted.

The looks I received were indifferent, a few nature-taking-its-course-type glances, and one or two looks that suggested I was being a pussy and should rid myself of a pro-life mindset. As they all turned back to witness the shameless execution, I grabbed hold of a bottle of Jack Daniels that lay on the counter to my right. I ripped it up high, choking its thick, sturdy neck of bulbous glass, and chugged—a good seven seconds. I removed it from my lips with a gasp and let out a frustrated growl. The music was high and so was I. Zeppelin's "When the Levee Breaks" began. On our way out of the kitchen, as I was wondering what category of oddities I would ingest next, Alison recognized three girls from her European history class—blonde, dirty-blonde, and bleached-blonde. Alison *sort of* went to school. That's how she was able to come to the States in the first place, majored in economics, I think. The girls were all foreign, dressed erotically, sexy—big tits, nice

legs, supple lips . . . and those accents. I told her to go hang with them, that I'd catch up with her, but then one of her friends pulled out a bag of cocaine. Bleached-blonde laid it out on the island next to the fruit bowl. Meddling with the oranges inside the fruit bowl was someone's wandering and neglected blue-fronted Amazon parrot. It was a green bird with blue feathers that wore a mini tailored leather jacket with cut-off sleeves . . . so its wings could fit through. I couldn't believe my eyes. You only see that kind of shit at the home of a godly rock icon in Hollywood, California.

"Drugs are bad," said the mystic bird.

"Fuck off," I said.

"Drugs are bad," said the bird.

"Is that all you can you say, bird?"

Alison and her foreign friends were laughing at me; at the same time, they were astonished at the sight of the leather-clad bird.

One of the blondes chimed in.

"You're an asshole," she said to the bird.

"You're an asshole," the bird said back.

"Can I get you a drink?" I asked the bird.

"Drugs are bad," the bird responded.

"Want some blow?" I asked.

"You're an asshole," said a different blonde to me jokingly.

I held a rolled-up dollar bill in front of its beak.

"You're an asshole," he said, then snatched my dollar and flew off.

"Hey, fucker," I said.

I followed the bird, left Alison behind. When I turned the corner, entering the living room, he was gone.

Little bastard owes me a buck.

The vast living room was cloaked in medieval history, walls covered with long tapestry, rich in dark golds, greens, and reds, dangling from the wooden ceiling beams like the fall of the Western Roman Empire. The room's low tone of light succeeded in hiding the true identities of the celebration's night crawlers. Bright lights at a party reveal too much truth in the ungodly hours, melting the masks of those pretending—which was everyone. A couple of the label guys called me over. They were talking to my bandmates, Avi, Tim, and Hector, selling hard a life in the fast lane.

"Your life is gonna change. You're gonna travel the world." Blah, blah, bale of bullshit. The next big band, they were certain we'd be. "Here, sign this . . . Sign that . . . Everything will be just fine."

Sure.

But I did want it to be true.

The label guys went on and on. I scanned the room, admired the decor. A vast sculpture of Penro riding a unicorn through a field of snakes sat in the middle of the room. Surrounding it was a pond full of koi fish. Entrance to the rock-and-roll giant's oversized coffin was that of a castle, a high archway filled in with heavy wooden doors, for he was a king. Just past the threshold stood an archetypal knight in shining armor equipped with a thick, antique broadsword that pierced the wooden belvedere it was planted on. You could almost feel the weight of the sword in your hands. It appeared to be watching over the place.

I wonder what Clive is doing?

I reached into my left jacket pocket. My bag of coke felt slim.

I wandered off, clocking the room for potential holders. I saw a familiar face roll in, B-Funk, and he never runs amok without the supporting surge of white dust.

"Jake, man, you guys fucking killed it tonight," he said.

"Thanks, brother," I said. "How'd you end up here?"

"Penro invited the whole fucking bar, plus my boy deals to him sometimes. I came with him."

"Speaking of which, you got any blow?"

Brandon smiled.

"The fuck you think?"

We hunted for the nearest bathroom to inhale the Peruvian chitchat. Two alluring women straight out of *Playboy* magazine—both brunettes, arm in arm—were on their way out of the commode as we were on our way in. They were wearing only their bras, each a pair of boxers, and long knee socks. Brandon and I turned to check out the babbling bunnies' backsides as they led each other down the hall. I closed and locked the door.

The bathroom was bigger than my apartment. To the right was a long hall, the walls dressed with expensive art hung crookedly, each painting odder than the last. The closer we came to the end of the hall, the darker the compositions arose. While in orientation they appeared to be portraits of great battles, the overall theme began to feel more satanic in nature with the victims expressing a state of hell on their faces, their beings gummed together, stressed in painted anguish—a suffering. The powder room was clad with stone walls and stained-glass windows that were finely detailed, and the archway to the toilet formed a delta shape. The counter was spacious and begging to be covered with delicious cocaine while dark-orange light fixtures kept the room low and warm. We were so far down the long hall that the noise from the party was barely a whisper. B-Funk broke out his bag and laid out four fat lines that we took down in a blink.

"This is good coke. Where'd you get it? Your boy?" I asked.

B-Funk seemed reluctant to answer.

"Umm, yeah, well, that's what I was talking about earlier. About Clive. That night I came by and dropped drugs off to him. The night he went down. My boy Roger hooked it up . . . so . . . you know . . . I feel terrible. I mean, I handed him the bag, ya know?" he said.

Everything stopped.

"Wait, what? What the fuck did you say?"

"About Clive?"

"No, what name did you just say? The guy you got the drugs from?"

"Roger?"

"Yeah, Roger. Black guy? Dated a girl from Denmark a while back, yeah?"

Heat began to spit from the pores in my face. I felt the veins in my neck bulging.

"Yeah . . . Wait, how did you know about Ali—" said Brandon.

"That motherfucker beats the shit out of women. You know that?" I asked.

"Are you talking about Alison?"

"That's exactly who the fuck I'm talking about."

The look on his face indicated that B-Funk began to add and subtract the data.

"Oh, shit . . . You're the Jake that she was talking about," he said, mostly to himself as he turned away from me, his thoughts trailing off.

He walked over to the toilet and sat with his face in his hands.

"What the fuck are you talking about? How the fuck do you know Alison?" I asked.

"I met her . . . at Roger's. They were fighting about some shit . . . I don't know . . . I didn't hear the whole thing. Something about some guy she was dating and that she was done with Roger and his bullshit. Roger was pretty pissed. I was at his place that night picking up some drugs for Clive but

I couldn't tell him they were for Clive because Roger's cousin had gotten into a fight with Clive back in his Miyagi's days. Clive fucked his cousin up pretty bad, so—"

"Get to the fucking point, Brandon."

"All right, all right." He continued on with his story, "So I told him . . . I told him the drugs were for you, Jake. But I had no idea that you were the guy Alison was talking about or that Roger even knew who you were. I didn't know it was you. I never would have told him the drugs were for you if I knew that."

"Wait, wait, wait . . . Alison told Roger about me?"

"Yeah. Like I said, I didn't catch the whole thing. I was just trying to get up outta there. But she was pretty revved up. Said she was done with him and was into this other dude . . . I guess . . . well . . . you."

"And he gave you drugs that night to give to me?"

"Right, but they were actually for Clive. That's what I was talking about earlier tonight. About Clive. I feel fucked up about it, Jake. I delivered the drugs to Clive that night. I feel kind of responsible."

"Did you know that that motherfucker keeps a bad batch on hand? Gives it to people who fuck with him. Alison told me. She's seen him do it."

"Wait, what? Oh, hell no . . . Jake, I would never . . . That shit is fucked up. No way I'd have any part of that bullshit. You know that."

I wasn't mad at B-Funk. I trusted him. He was a good friend, and he respected Clive, knew him longer than I had.

"It's not your fault, B. Besides, Clive is fine now, and when I tell him what the fuck is going on, all hell is gonna break loose," I said.

B-Funk looked at me like I was bats in the belfry. I think the combination of my pure hatred toward Roger and all the cocaine that I had just ingested made me look crazy. I'm not, though.

"Wait, what? Jake, what do you mean, tell Cli—"

"B, tell me you weren't there when Roger hit her. Please tell me you weren't there."

"Fuck no, Jake. I swear, when I left she was still there packing up some of her shit. They were yelling at each other, but he didn't put a hand on her."

The backs of my eyeballs turned into a theater of memories, of puzzle pieces—Alison's face, Clive lying on the bathroom floor, Roger smiling.

That motherfucker gave Clive bad drugs thinking they were gonna be for me. Clive's overdose was because of me, because of Roger.

B-Funk started to back away, hands out to the side. He could see the eruption inside of me rising to the top.

"Jake, I'm so sorry, man," he said.

I took a step toward him.

"Where's Roger?"

BAD COCAINE

THE NIGHT CLIVE overdosed—six months ago—started with a knock at the door. I was getting ready for work so I ignored it.

Clive'll get it.

When I got out of the shower, I heard the door close. I finished getting ready, had a smoke, read a few pages of Elmore Leonard's *Get Shorty*. The apartment was quiet. It was almost six in the evening, had to be to work at six thirty. I went to the kitchen, threw back a shot of vodka—ritual work preparation.

"Later, mate," I said.

Clive didn't respond. On my way out the door, I realized I didn't have my ID card for work.

Where the fuck did I leave it? Oh, that's right, last night I was cutting up lines in Clive's room.

"Mate, can you toss me my Lux card?" I asked, standing outside his door.

No response.

"Clive . . ."

Again, no response.

I knocked, then opened the door. I looked to my right, no Clive. There was leftover cocaine from the night before on the end table, so I fingered it and rubbed my gums. I noticed the hue of yellow light shadowing off the wall across from the bathroom.

"You taking a shit?" I asked.

I turned the corner, saw Clive's feet sticking out of the doorway. He still had his socks on. I rushed to the door, pulled it open. Clive lay on his side, unconscious, blood dripping from his nose and down the side of his face, white foam hanging from his lips. He lay too still.

"*Clive!*" I shouted.

I dropped to my knees, turned him over, and slapped the sides of his face.

"No, no, no . . . C'mon, Clive," I said.

He wouldn't respond. I slapped him again. I shook him. Nothing worked. I pulled out my cell phone and called 911.

"Nine-one-one, what is your emergency?" asked a calm voice, a woman.

"I need help. I need an ambulance. My friend won't wake up. He's on the floor. He's not waking up . . ." I said.

"What's your name?"

I told her my name, gave her the address and the code to get in.

"What number are you calling from?" she asked.

I gave her my number.

"He's not waking up," I said.

"Try to stay calm, Jake. We're sending EMTs to you right away. Can you tell me what happened?" said the calm voice.

"I went into his room and found him lying on the bathroom floor on his side. He's bleeding."

"Where is he bleeding?"

"From his nose."

"Is he breathing?"

Clive lay peacefully, clean. There was nothing connected to him. No machines, no wires. I brought the covers up higher to his chest.

"That's better," I said.

I thought about Clive's parents. I was afraid to talk to them. They'd partially blame me. I couldn't call my mother, couldn't tell her what happened. She'd worry. So would my brother. They'd wonder what kind of a life I'd been living, ask too many questions, questions I didn't want to answer. I wished my dad were there. He was good in the deep, good with perspective and insight. I could have used a little play-them-as-they-lay-type pep talk. Dad was good at making me laugh, too. He could turn dark into light. I still had his old phone number but it was no longer his. The last time I tried to call it, some old lady answered.

"Wrong number, young man. Is there something I can do for you, dear?" she said.

But I still called from time to time.

"Gotta stay strong, my friend," I said to Clive.

His stillness was a contradiction. Clive was a moving part in the world. Rapid and erratic, an uncontrollable mass. He inspired emotion like no one I'd ever known—anger, hate, love, lust. A fighter, and it now looked like the fight in him had died. Someone needed to fight for him like the many times he'd fought for me. I owed him that much. And he owed it to me to stay alive. I could keep him alive.

"Just gotta ride this one out, man. Yut . . . gonna be just fine, my friend," I said.

Clive changed my life, made it more exciting, showed me how to face my fears—my evolution through the gift of his friendship, my actions more free of cost. For better or for worse, I needed that. And I loved him for bringing that out of me. He told me to write about the past, my life, things I didn't necessarily want to talk about at parties. He said to tell the truth through my music. I pressed his hand against my forehead, thought about the good times, praying for the best of times yet to come.

After my visit with Clive at the hospital, I snuck out the back stairwell. I knew his parents would be there soon. The nurses never even saw me. I went back to the apartment, tried to remember where Clive would hide the drugs. I was privy to his favorite spots—atop the doorframe to his room, in a teacup in the highest, deepest part of the cabinet, and about nine other spots. I gathered up as much as I could find and hoped there was no more. I packed a bag and went down to the Motel 6 a block away, paid the thirty-five dollars with a credit card. The motel had roaches, but it was better than hanging around for the cops to search the place. I went out to the bank and drained my account, almost four hundred bucks. I bought some bread and peanut butter and jelly. I came back to the hotel, put my bag down on the bed, took a pull off a fifth of Jim, and pulled out a pipe and a rock. I lit it and smoked it. Such euphoria! Your energy spikes and your insides are cloud-like. I did that for three days, no sleep, drank water from the faucet.

I paced and paced, thought about Clive. I figured after he got himself right he'd probably have to go to some rehab for a time, a week or two maybe. He'd play the part, go to the meetings, talk about how drugs are bad, and blah, blah, bag-a-dicks. But they wouldn't be able to help him. He'd have to convince his family that he was okay to leave the facility, tell them that he'd had a new lease on life and all that. He'd convince them that he would look forward to living an extremely dull and deathly boring existence that was void of any real living. He'd tell them what they wanted to hear.

After three days I still hadn't heard from Clive. I called him a few times—no answer. His parents and the stiffs at the rehab clinic probably wouldn't let him talk to anybody, especially enablers, which I would surely be considered. I grew impatient, worried that maybe his family had taken him back East, made him cut ties with me. I couldn't stand not knowing, so I mustered up the guts to call his mother. A man answered the phone, his stepfather, George. I'd spoken to him on the phone before. Nice guy. Clive got along fine with him, but they weren't close.

"H-hello, may I speak to Clive?" I asked, trying to disguise my voice.

"Who's calling?" he asked.

I didn't answer.

"Jake? Is that you, Jake?"

I couldn't answer. I couldn't.

"Jake, Leena and I wanted to come by, pick up Clive's thi—"

I hung up, locked the door behind me, drank more whiskey, smoked more cocaine, paced some more, bit my nails till they bled. I was afraid to go back to the apartment.

What if Clive's parents are there? They're gonna blame me. I know it.

I couldn't sleep. I couldn't eat. I lost track of the days. My life felt as empty as my gut and my head visited more than a few alternate realties. Outside my window there were crows swarming the sky, surrounding the motel, must have been a hundred of them. I closed the curtain, put my back against the wall. Occasionally I'd feel a gentle tap on my shoulder. I'd turn around abruptly, frightened. Nobody was there. I turned off the lights, curled up in a blanket, huddled in the corner of the room farthest from the door and window.

What if he never comes back?

Then a knock at the door, a familiar knock. I could barely stand. The walls carried me to the door. I looked through the peephole. Nothing. No one.

"Who's there?" I asked.

No answer.

I dropped to my knees, prayed for Clive to come back. Then another knock. I looked through the peephole. Again, there was no one. Frustrated, I yanked the door open. And there was Clive, alive as can be.

"What it look like?"

2:00 AM – AUGUST 14

I CAME OUT of Penro's bathroom a hunter. I told B-Funk to leave the party. He was so visibly distraught by the sum of our conversation that he complied without question. He told me to be careful—a clear warning to the danger that comes along with confronting a guy like Roger. I didn't care.

"Jake . . . we still need to talk about Clive," said B-Funk before he left.

I walked away. All I could think about was Roger. That motherfucker tried to kill me and *almost* killed Clive. I needed to know what the fiendish drug dealer looked like. I needed to find him. That's what Clive would do. I called Clive but his number wasn't working.

Must not have paid his bill again.

"Dammit, Clive. Why the fuck are you not here right now?" I asked no one.

I walked into a crowd of people forming a circle in the living room—they were cheering something on. As I pushed my way through the circle, I saw Penro dressed in his knight's armor, the one by the front door. All except the helmet. He was engaged in a mock sword fight with some other guy I didn't recognize because *he* was wearing the knight's helmet. Normally

I would grab a chair and enjoy such drunken debauchery, but I needed to find Alison. I needed to know what Roger looked like. I clocked her on the other side of the circle. I slid through the cluster of greasy patrons, grabbed hold of Alison, pulled her out of the circle and over toward the front door.

"Does Roger know about me?" I asked.

"What the fuck, Jake!" she said.

"Did you tell him about me?"

She was afraid.

"Yes . . ."

"What did you tell him?"

She began to cry.

"That I loved you."

"What?"

In the throes of such anger and frustration, her words made me feel better than I had in a long time.

"He was trying to get me back. I went over there to get some of my stuff, clothes and stuff. He told me he loved me and wanted me back. I said no. I told him . . . that I loved you."

"You said that?"

"Yes!"

"Then why the fuck did you leave that day at my house? Why didn't you come back?"

"Because you scared me, Jake. You were acting crazy . . . like him."

It was hard for me to argue her point.

"Did you know he gave my friend Brandon drugs that night . . . to give to me?" I asked.

"No. Wait, why? Jake, I don't understand. Who's Brandon?"

"He's a friend. He deals coke for Roger. Brandon was picking up drugs for me the night you broke it off with Roger, but the coke was actually for my roommate, Clive. Brandon couldn't tell Roger that they were for Clive, so he said they were for me."

Alison shook her head, her face curled in confusion. I continued.

"It's a long story. Never mind. That's not important."

"Jake, I don't understand. What does this have to do wi—"

"Alison, Clive overdosed that night," I said. "From the drugs that Roger thought he was giving to me."

Her face uncurled.

She realized what Roger had done. It all started to crash down on her, on me, on us.

"Jake, I'm sorry. I didn't know. I'm so so—" she said.

Alison stopped short and looked over my shoulder. She put her hand to her mouth and backed away in fear.

I looked over toward the entryway.

"Is that him?" I asked.

She didn't answer. The music was loud.

"*Is that him?*" I said.

She nodded.

"Please don't, Jake. You don't know him. He's dangerous."

I didn't respond, just stared. I thought about Clive. About him lying there on the bathroom floor, helpless, lifeless. All the anger that I'd held inside of me, from my whole life, it filled me, all the betrayals, all the letdowns. I thought of Kenny, of backstabbing Greg Dogard, of Nicole and Wayne Decanter, of my parents' dismissal of the lion's ill intentions, of my father's infidelities and of his absence, of Ray and Peter's abandonment, of all the times that I wasn't loved enough. I thought and I thought and I waited for my anger to overtake my fears. Penro and his pal had dropped their swords and were now blowing lines off a copy of *The Great Gatsby* that sat on a desk in the corner of the main room. Penro was still wearing his armor. He motioned for me to join him. I didn't respond. All I saw was

Roger and the sword that was leaning against the bar. I looked down to see that it was now in my hands, its weight empowering. When I looked up, Roger was gone and Alison was still trying to stop me.

"You need to leave," I said.

"Please, Jake, come with me," she pleaded.

"Alison, you need to go . . . *now.*"

She left in tears, and I went searching for Roger. The broadsword hung loosely from my right hand. My heart was beating fast, the bass of each beat shaking my entire body. When I turned the corner, I saw Roger and his lackey down the hall next to the bathroom. I watched as he handed something to one of the partygoers in exchange for cash. I walked toward them, down the hall, stalking my prey, trembling with fear and rage. My chest rose to twice the size with the depth of each heavy breath, my heart beat faster with every stride. My footsteps were only feelings, not sounds. They entered the bathroom. The hallway was clear. No one would see me enter behind them. Without a break in my gait, I found myself in front of the bathroom door. I stood there for a moment, realizing what I was about to do. Second thoughts began to state their case.

I can't turn back after this.

I backed away from the door, up against the hall across the way, felt the cool marble kiss the back of my neck while I focused on the doorknob, contemplating my intentions. But then, I thought again—about Clive, near death, lying on the bathroom floor. I thought about my best friend, the one I'd looked for my whole life and finally found, the one who'd never leave. I thought about my loyalty to him, and his toward me. My eyes filled from the fear and the rage.

What would Clive do? He'd be loyal. He'd take this sword and bash Roger's skull in. I wish you were here, Clive.

I took a deep breath, reached into the breast of my right outside jacket pocket, and pulled out Clive's flask. I took the last sip of whiskey, pulled out the remainder of my cocaine, and emptied it on the end table made of thick oak that rested against the wall. I aggressively snorted the drugs, snuffing out my emotions, and reengaged in my acrimony. With the heavy blade hanging from my right hand, the fine tip piercing the stone floor, I put my cold left hand on the warm doorknob and turned.

For Clive.

2:41 AM – AUGUST 14

I HURRIED OUT of the bathroom, went through Penro's kitchen and out the back door, past the guest house, and into some bushes behind some trees. I crouched down low, slowed my breath, trying to stay quiet. I still had the sword in my hands. It wasn't that sharp but it was strong enough to cave a man's head in. There was blood on the blade, on my clothes, too. A couple of Roger's lackeys were rummaging around the side yard where the cars were parked.

They must have found him.

"What's he look like?" one of them said.

"Fuck, man, I don't know. White guy, had on a white T-shirt. That's all I saw when he came out of the bathroom," said the other.

"How bad is Roger?"

"Bad, man. Fucked him up real bad."

"And Zeke?"

"Same."

"Cops gonna be here, man. We gotta get the fuck outta here."

I was about fifty feet away from them, ready to swing the heavy blade if they found me. Everyone at the party must have discovered the horrific red scene I left behind because people were piling out fast. Girls were screaming, some crying. The cops would indeed be coming soon. I had to act fast without being seen. I heard something rummaging up behind me. I turned around, still crouched, holding the sword in both hands like a samurai. I saw a figure walking toward me.

"What the fuck?" I said.

"Yaaboy!"

Clive?

"Dude, what the fuck are you doing here?" I whispered, motioning him to get down.

"Relax," he said. "They can't see me," he continued.

"I'm not taking the chance. Get down."

He casually knelt down.

"Jake, what the fuck are we dealing with here?"

My voice was shaky, desperate, afraid.

"I think I fucked up, Clive. But I had to. It's nothing you wouldn't have done . . . I had t—"

"Is he dead?"

"Is who dead?"

"Elvis, asshole . . . Who the fuck do you think? Is Roger dead?"

"I don't know . . . Wait . . . How the fuck did you know it was Roger?"

As I was trying to figure out, first, why Clive was here, and second, how the fuck he knew about Roger, I saw a car pull up, a nice one. A 1967 Charger, metallic blue. Whoever it was bolted out of the car toward the house and left his keys in it, the car still running. The coast was clear, so Clive and I hopped in and peeled out of the driveway.

Maybe there is a God. Who else would give me this many chances?

I drove, kept looking in the rearview mirror to see if we were being followed. I thought about Niki Fine from work. I was supposed to meet up with her after Promise's birthday party. I looked at my phone. She'd called twice.

I should have gone to meet her tonight. I wouldn't be in this mess.

"Anyone see you?" Clive asked.

"No . . . I don't think so. Maybe the back of me. Not my face. Alison will know, but she won't say anything. She loves me."

I smiled for a moment. Clive looked at me as if I was absolutely wrong about how Alison felt about me.

"B-Funk will put two and two together, but he'd never rat," I continued.

Clive appeared to agree.

"I had to do it, mate. That night . . . Roger gave us bad drugs . . . I mean, gave *you* bad drugs, but they were meant for me. I found out from B-Funk and Alison. I mean, they had no idea, but I put it together with some things B said and what Alison told me. Alison loves me. She told Roger that. B told Roger the drugs were for me because he couldn't tell them they were for you because you fucked his cousin up at Miyagi's. So Roger thought he was trying to fuck with *me* by giving me bad drugs, but *you* bought the drugs, so . . . Fuck . . . He tried to fucking kill us, man."

I realized I was crying.

"I know," said Clive.

"You know? What do you mean you know? How the fuck do you know? What the fuck are you not telling me? What the fuck is going on? My conversation with B-Funk earlier tonight at Reggie's . . . What the fuck was that all about?"

"You already know, Jake."

"Stop playing fucking ga—"

"Make sure you're not being followed. Ditch the car in the next side street . . . Cab home."

We were on Santa Monica Boulevard. I turned down Genesee and parked.

"Wipe the steering wheel clean."

I grabbed a napkin from the glove box, wiped the steering wheel clean, the door handles as well. I still had the sword.

"Wipe the sword and throw it in the sewer."

I wiped the sword and shoved it down a sewer a half a block away.

"What now?"

"Hail a cab."

I flagged one down on Santa Monica and got in.

"Take us to 6550 Yucca Street, please," I said.

"Are we waiting for someone else?" asked the driver.

"No," I said.

I closed the door. The cab didn't move. The driver was staring at me in the rearview.

"What the fuck are you waiting for?" I said.

The driver stopped staring and hit the gas. Clive and I remained quiet in the cab as the night's events replayed in my head. I wanted it all to be another one of my bad dreams. Lately, there'd been many . . . bad dreams. Like the one with Patrick Thornberg and Debbie from Kansas (Reggie's old roommate).

I was in Debbie's bathroom, washing my hands. I looked in the mirror. Debbie's bedroom door wasn't fully closed. In the mirror's reflection I could see the left side of her face and the right side of Patrick's. He looked scared.

"Everyone knows you're fucking gay, Patrick. Stop pretending like you're not," said Debbie, in full command of the room, her tone void of all remorse, her conviction doused in hate. Patrick nervously tried to de-escalate the situation.

"Debbie . . . please, keep your voice down."

"Don't tell me to keep my voice down . . . you fucking fag," said Debbie.

"I don't want to talk about this anymore," said Patrick.

Most people who knew him figured Patrick was gay. Nobody cared—dime a dozen. This was Hollywood. But Patrick wasn't ready to admit it, and he didn't have to. But Debbie kept pushing.

What the fuck does she care?

"I can't believe I let you stick your dick inside of me. You're disgusting . . . and a fucking liar," she said.

Aha!

Debbie was old school, thought the gays were sinners and whatnot; she was a bigot. As I stood outside of her room, peering through the slit that revealed her venomous right-wing posture, the water still running in the sink, I became angry . . . for Patrick. I wanted him to stand up for himself as she rifled through a list of verbal daggers:

"It's not natural."

"You're a sinner . . . the devil."

"You're going straight to hell."

I wanted to kick open the door, tell her to shut the fuck up, to leave the poor bastard alone. Nobody deserved to be treated that way. Debbie swarmed him like a school of fire ants, moved closer to his face, nose to nose, snarling, creating a fog in his line of sight with the breath of her single-mindedness, beating him to death with degrading words. She looked like she wanted to eat him. She looked like a lion, and Patrick looked like an eight-year-old boy, frozen with fear.

This isn't my problem.

As I turned away to leave, to mind my own business, I heard a muffled sound. I went back to the door, saw Patrick's lower legs, toes to the floor. Debbie's legs were toes up underneath him. The sound was desperate, like Debbie was trying to speak with a pillow over her face, or someone's hands around her throat.

Probably fucking . . . ha . . . Make-up sex.

I heard a crash. It didn't sound like make-up sex anymore. I opened the door. Patrick had snapped. He was on top, choking her. He was red, she was purple—like a fire truck running over a beet. Veins protruded from his neck and forearms while Debbie's life was slipping away. I watched. Debbie turned toward me, caught me staring, her bulging eyes announcing her terror. Patrick, blinded by his lust for Debbie's demise, didn't notice me. All he saw was a death, a solution. I stood behind him, the back of his shirt soaked with sweat. "Let It Be" played at a medium volume. I turned it up as Debbie's heels scraped the rug . . . I felt like God. I thought of Kenny Harris, picturing my hands around his throat, then around Debbie's, then Greg's, then Roger's. I watched as Debbie withered away. Her struggle weakened, the kicking slowed. But this wasn't Kenny, this wasn't the same.

God wouldn't let this happen . . . would he?

I grabbed Patrick, tossed him to the side, startling him back to his fearful frame; in his wicked rage he had dismissed all things around him. Debbie grabbed at her throat and rolled over to the corner of the room next to the window. She tried to catch her breath. Patrick was shaking, crying. He sat on the floor near Debbie's bed, knees to his chest, his arms wrapped around them like the ribbon on a gift. I took a step toward him. He thought I was going to hit him, so he put his hands up in defense, closed his eyes, and turned his face away to the side. I could see that he'd urinated all over himself. So did Debbie. The whole room now smelled like piss and hate.

"Patrick. It's over . . . it's okay," I said.

He said nothing.

"You need to get the fuck out of here," I said.

He hesitated, looked blank, unresponsive, so I crouched down to his level.

"*Patrick! Look at me!* You need to go . . . *now!*" I said.

Debbie's breathing calmed, her face no longer purple, more the color of a pale rose. She was frightened, appalled. Some of that was for me.

Patrick got up and ran, left the bedroom, left the party.

"Are you happy now?" I said to Debbie.

There was no sympathy in my voice.

"Why the f-f-fuck w-w-were you just st-st-standing there?" she stuttered.

I walked over with cold intent. She looked at me like a rabbit looks at a hawk. I dropped to a knee. She recoiled.

"Because . . . you f-f-fucking deserved it, you c-c-cunt," I said.

My lack of sympathy, my outright cruelty toward her, it changed the shape of her face.

"And if you ever tell anyone about this . . ." I began, then leaned in closer.

She turned her face to the side, closed her eyes, her hands still protecting her throat.

"If you ever tell anyone about this, about Patrick . . . I'll fucking kill you," I said.

I got up and walked out, leaving Debbie alone in the corner, almost a carcass. And that was the end of the dream.

The cab stopped at our apartment, and I couldn't stop thinking about Patrick and Debbie.

"How much?" I asked the driver.

"Twenty seventy," he said.

Clive and I got out and walked toward the building. I turned to see the driver staring at us again, all the way to the front door.

"What the fuck is he looking at?" I asked Clive.

"You. Because you sound like a crazy person," he said.

"Fuck you."

We got in the elevator.

"It wasn't a dream, Jake," said Clive.

"What the fuck are you talking about? What wasn't a dream?" I asked.

"Patrick . . . and Debbie . . . that wasn't a dream."

"How did you . . . What the f—"

"That's why Debbie left Hollywood so fast. She left that night at Reggie's, the night you almost let Patrick choke her out. That's why she went back to Kansas. 'Cause of you, psycho."

Clive continued, told me that Patrick disappeared that night as well. Cops found his body in a ravine in Runyon Canyon some months later. They called it suicide. But Debbie had verbally and emotionally annihilated him that night. She all but put the pills in his body and pushed him off the cliff. Poor Patrick couldn't deal with the possibility of people knowing who he really was. He'd been lying for all those years, to himself, to his family, to his friends, until he couldn't lie anymore, until someone had found out his secrets. That shit catches up to you.

The elevator stopped. I was light-headed, dizzy. I used my hands to catch my balance—that filthy elevator. I hadn't slept in four days, the booze, the drugs, the violence. I was starting to feel the effects of my life. The doors opened and I walked out.

"Clive," I said.

He didn't answer. I couldn't see him. My vision started to blur, so I leaned against the wall, slid my way toward our apartment. I saw a hand stick a key in the door. It was Clive. I could tell because I noticed the red leather band on his wrist. We turned the key, then came the darkest shade of night.

RENT IS PAST DUE

PEOPLE HAVE THE audacity to pretend that the bad things don't affect them, that stepping in the dog shit of life only requires that we wipe the shit off. We pretend we're bulletproof . . . for a time. But, in reality, we're soft, uncertain human beings, forcing ourselves to play a role we imagine people want to see. Nobody really knows what they're doing. It's all an illusion, of safety, of control. We act like upstanding citizens only when people are looking. We do things that are noble. We behave in such a way that makes us appear kind. It's purely survival. We're all hiding, because that smell of shit never goes away. It sticks to the bottom of our souls forever. And it's tiresome . . . to pretend.

"Wake up, motherfucker."

I felt a kick. It woke me. I sat up in bed, opened my eyes, looked right, then left. No Clive. I was alone. There were no half-naked brunettes lying across me wearing only socks. My head was pounding. My mouth was dry. I caught a glimpse of myself in the closet mirror. I was wearing the same clothes I'd had on at Penro's, bloodstains on my shirt and my hands. I got up to check Clive's room—he wasn't there. My whole body hurt. I couldn't eat. My mind was ripping out of my skull, pulsating like an infected toe. The little bit of sunlight peeking through the side of my curtains was blinding, so I stapled them to the wall. A few times our landlord knocked on the door calling for rent. We were two months behind on my end. Clive's watch rested on my milk-crate end table. I checked it—I'd slept for thirty hours. My cell phone was off, battery was dead. I didn't want to plug it in. The home phone kept ringing, at least fifty times. The voicemails were mostly from my mother, some from my brother, some from B-Funk, some from the Grand Lux Cafe, my bandmates, Alison, Niki, Brian, and Matty. But I had no idea where Clive was. I didn't want to talk to anyone until I spoke to Clive, especially not my mother. She would have heard the truth in my voice.

I tried to piece it together, my night at Penro's. I thought of how Roger had begged, and that things had really gone to shit. My home phone rang, went to voicemail. It was my mother. She was crying this time and begging for me to call her back. I couldn't pick it up.

Do I call her back? What do I say? She's worried sick. I have to call her back. I'll just pretend like everything is fine, but that I'm late for work . . . Yeah, a quick call to let her know I'm alive.

I dragged myself out of bed and grabbed the home phone to call my mother back. It rang as soon as I touched it. I put the phone to my ear.

"Hello," I said.

It was Clive's mother. I hadn't spoken to her since right after Clive overdosed.

"Hello . . . Hello . . . Jake? Is that you?" she asked.

Her voice was soft and motherly. Mine was shaky.

"Hey . . . Mrs. Salton. H-how are you?" I asked.

"I'm okay, Jake. We're getting along okay. How are *you*, Jake?"

"I'm okay . . . I guess."

"You sound tired."

"Yeah . . ."

There was silence.

"Jake, I've spoken to your mother. She's very worried about you. You need to give her a call."

"I will. I promise."

"Listen, Jake, I'm calling because George and I can no longer help out with the rent. We knew how hard it was on you, so we promised the six months . . . but it's just too much for us. I'm sorry we can't do more. Oh, I hope you understand."

There was a knock at the door. The landlord again.

"Umm, rent, Mrs. Salton? Hang on a sec."

Knock! Knock! Knock!

"Yeah, hang on a minute," I shouted at the door.

I turned my attention back to the phone.

"Jake, is everything okay?"

"Ah, yeah, it's fine, just someone at the door. What did you mean pay re—"

The knocking became louder, more rapid.

"Hang on," I shouted. "Mrs. Salton, I don't understand. Do you know where Clive is?" I asked.

Knock! Knock! Knock!

I couldn't take it anymore. I snapped. I bolted for the door, put the phone to my thigh to mask the sound, and hurled the door open.

"*Fuck off!*" I said.

The force of my voice threw the small Cambodian man— my landlord—back against the door across the hall. He looked down at the bloodstains on my shirt, then back to my face. My eyes must have insinuated that he should run, because he did. I shut the door and put the phone back to my ear. Mrs. Salton had hung up, so I hung up. The phone rang again immediately. I didn't answer, let it go to voicemail. It was Clive's stepfather.

"Jake . . . Jake . . . It's George. What the hell is going on over there? Jake?"

I ripped the phone out of the wall, and within seconds an impartial flood came crashing into my apartment, rising to the ceiling as fast as it arrived, turning the entire apartment into a fishbowl. Taking on water, I couldn't breathe. Panicked, I swam to the ceiling, scratching at the stucco to bore a hole in hopes of relieving the pressure. I counted my last seconds and closed my eyes.

When I opened my eyes, the water was not there. I was lying on the floor, my back to the shag, soaked in my own sweat. My empty gut was shriveling like an angry raisin, eating at itself. I clenched my fists, closed my eyes as tight as I could, trying to squeeze the pain away while a thousand voices cried inside.

Death punch.

Parents have the tendency to tell their kids that everything's going to be okay. It was the answer to all of life's problems. I wondered if I'd be lucky enough someday to have the same power of knowing that they had. Time passed and I got older, yet I never achieved such powers. Still, I would hear others spout the same mostly generic lie—myself included. I'd been programmed to believe it was true. And then one day the phone rings and everything is not okay.

After my conversation with Clive's mother, I was frozen, staring up at the ceiling, praying that Clive would come back again, like he had at the motel last time. He'd help me get out of this mess, this thing with Roger. I saw a white piece of paper on the floor by the door, sat up, picked up the letter. It was an eviction notice. It said I had thirty days to get out. I wasn't going to last another thirty minutes. The phone was still on the floor. Next to the phone was a pile of mail. On top was an envelope addressed to me. It was from my mother. I stared at it for a moment and went back into my bedroom. I loaded the pipe with a white rock and listened to the crackle as my body lifted . . . ever so briefly. I gripped the bottle of Jack Daniels that lay on my plastic shelving unit and hit it hard for six seconds, then walked back out to the living room and grabbed the envelope. I was equal parts wired and drained, mentally and physically. My hands trembled and my heart bounced as I opened the letter. It was a card. A check for fifty bucks fell out, and there was a note.

Dear Jake,

Happy birthday, hon. Please call. I haven't heard from you in a while, sweetie. I hope all is well. I'd just like to hear that you are doing okay. You know how much I worry about you. I miss you and I love you. I wish so much for you to be happy, Jake. Hope the money helps. Next week is your father's anniversary. I can't believe it has been ten years . . .

That night, when I last spoke to my father, when I was thirteen, I laid in bed after Regina Hayward's party feeling guilty about the way I'd treated him and about skipping the weekend with him. Rene Teller, the girl I was in love with at the time, my reason for going to the party in the first place, kissed Greg that night—that son of a bitch. Before falling asleep I prayed to God that Greg would fall down some stairs and that my father would forgive me. And in my dreams my father did. But then I was startled awake by a loud, unusual cry. I shook off the cobwebs, popped out of bed, and opened my door, breathing as if I'd run up and down the stairs a thousand times. The crying doubled in volume as I entered the hall. I was standing in front of my mother's bedroom door. I opened it quickly. My brother was down on his knees, cradled in my mother's arms. Stan was on the other side of the bed, facing the opposite wall, his back to me. He was holding his head in his hands, staring down at the floor.

"What's wrong?" I asked.

I didn't really want to know.

Mom couldn't help crying as she tried to console my brother. She looked up at me, eyes puffy and watered, her face flush and weary.

"It's your dad . . . H-he's . . . He's had a heart attack," she said.

Before my brain could calculate the sum of her words, the tears came, I began to shake, and my lips curled in toward my teeth. Stan turned around; his face sagged, so tired. Such a phone call can change the way a person looks.

"He's all right, right?" I asked.

No answer.

"H-he's all right, right?" I asked again.

Mom tried, but still nothing.

"*Mom . . .*"

She motioned for me to come to her. I refused. I wanted her to answer me first. I wanted to know that everything would be okay, that my dad was okay. I needed to know that I would see him again, that I could say I'm sorry. I needed to tell him how much I loved him.

"Tell me he's all right," I said. "Please . . . tell me—" I continued.

"I'm sorry, baby . . . H-he's gone . . . I'm so sorry," she said.

I'd broken my father's heart, and it killed him.

The reality of my mother's letter hit like a hammer, crashing into my cranial vortex like an emotional, psychological, and physical blitzkrieg. A three-on-one assault on my entire world. It wasn't a fair fight, but I suppose it was one that I started a long time ago. I'm surprised that it took this long to find me. I wasn't ready. I should have listened to my father. He once told me how important it was to be prepared.

"Noah built the ark *before* the storm, Jakey boy," he said.

But it was too late.

So this is what a nervous breakdown feels like.

I grabbed the bottle of Jack, took a heavy pull, then hit the pipe. I kept feeding rocks into the glass cylinder until the entire bag was gone. Four grams is a lot of crack to smoke in just thirty minutes, but I longed to be swept away. I put the last rock in. My hands were shaking. I couldn't hold them still enough to bring the pipe to my lips. The pipe and lighter fell to the ground as I convulsed my way over to the closet, slamming against the wall—it was the only place I could bear to be, my cubby. My white T-shirt was still stained with Roger's blood, my polyester pants wrinkled and layered with grime. I slid the door shut. The left side of my body tightened. My teeth clenched, jaw locked in place, leaving no room to breathe. My legs went numb, and like Frosty the fucking Snowman, I melted into the carpet. A sharp pain in my brain, a dagger, it closed my eyes. And there it was again . . . Death punch.

SAME AS YOU

I WOKE TO the sound of the ocean, could smell it, too. All the tears and blood had been lifted from my white T-shirt. It was dry and bright, and my polyester pants were pressed and fresh. I picked myself up off the floor, feeling oddly energetic and healthy, and stepped out of the closet. My room had been cleaned, my bed made, too.

"What the fuck?" I said to no one.

I opened the door and walked outside of my bedroom. A bright light washed over my line of sight. For a moment I was blind. I felt my toes sinking into the warm sand as my eyes began to adjust from the pitch-black of my closet to the bright sun of a new day. Straight ahead, about a hundred feet, was an outdoor bar with a long tiki roof. I could smell piña coladas—they were rather easy to breathe in. The bar looked as empty as the beach. I walked through the sand, my bare feet appreciating each step. I went around to the front of the place, facing the water. There was a sign above the bar that read: *Tamboo Tavern, Welcome to Rincón, Puerto Rico*. A beautiful view, the smell, the sound, everything was fortunate.

I know this place.

My dad used to talk about this bar. He'd come here on his business trips.

"It looks like a dream, but it's real," he'd say.

While staring at the ocean, I was turned by the sound of a blender's blades cutting through chunks of ice like a mini chainsaw. Sitting at the end of the bar was Clive . . . and . . . my father. The two of them were wrapped in conversation like they had known each other for many years, old war buddies talking about the time that one saved the other's life, pulled him out of a foxhole or some shit. They looked over at me, both nodded as if I was expected but late to the party.

"Ummm . . . what the fuck?" I said.

They both smiled.

"Hey, Jake. Piña colada?" my dad asked.

Clive lifted his glass, tilted his head, and raised his eyes. Cheshire Clive!

"Yaaboy," he said.

"Okay, now I know this is a dream. Since when do the two of you drink piña coladas?"

I turned toward the bar.

"I'll take a whiskey," I said, looking for the bartender.

"Here, try it," said Clive, handing me his glass.

Suddenly the bartender was pushing a freshly made piña colada toward me, looked right into my eyes, said nothing, then walked away. He was an older gentleman, fatherly. He was daunting, white hair, eyes of gold, moved with grace. It turned out to be a pretty good piña colada, I must admit.

"Soooo, what the fuck are we doing here, guys? Why am I dreaming about the three of us hanging out at a Puerto Rican beach? Beautiful place, but what gives?" I asked.

"And what if it's not a dream, Jakey boy?" asked my dad.

I looked into his eyes, saw mine.

"I miss you, Dad. I'm so sorry."

"It's okay, son."

"I should have never gone to that party that night. I should have come to see you . . . like we planned. Things would've been different. You'd still be alive."

"You didn't kill me, Jake. It was just my time. It had nothing to do with you. It's very important that you understand that."

Clive just sat and listened, comforting the situation with his presence.

"I was such an asshole to you that day on the phone, though. You didn't deserve that, Dad. Please, forgive me."

"Jake, I've already forgiven you. I forgave you that day."

He rested his hand on my shoulder.

"It wasn't your fault, Jake," he said.

I grabbed my father, hugged him. It had been ten years since I'd felt that. It was exactly the way I remembered it. We shared stories, laughed. Stories of my father's younger days, stories that my dad and I told Clive, stories Clive and I told to Dad. It all felt connected, the best moment of my life. I thought of nothing else. There was only us, and there was only right here, right now. I'd never felt such peace. I turned to Clive.

"So what the fuck are you doing here?" I asked.

"Same as you," he said.

GRAND PATRONS

INKSHARES

INKSHARES is a reader-driven publisher and producer based in Oakland, California. Our books are selected not by a group of editors, but by readers worldwide.

While we've published books by established writers like *Big Fish* author Daniel Wallace and *Star Wars: Rogue One* scribe Gary Whitta, our aim remains surfacing and developing the new author voices of tomorrow.

Previously unknown Inkshares authors have received starred reviews and been featured in The *New York Times*. Their books are on the front tables of Barnes & Noble and hundreds of independents nationwide, and many have been licensed by publishers in other major markets. They are also being adapted by Oscar-winning screenwriters at the biggest studios and networks.

Interested in making your own story a reality? Visit Inkshares.com to start your own project or find other great books.

CPSIA information can be obtained
at www.ICGtesting.com
Printed in the USA
FSHW021534171019
63095FS